HELLFIRE PASS

It had taken ten years for Sundance to find the men who had murdered his family during the Civil War. It came unexpectedly and he wasn't quite ready for it, but soon the fires of vengeance were burning strongly inside him. However, he hadn't counted on the hostility that still existed towards Johnny Rebs in the north. Nevertheless, he was prepared for the men who came after him, and he was the one leading the killing this time.

HANK J. KIRBY

HELLFIRE PASS

Complete and Unabridged

LINFORD
Leicester

First published in Great Britain in 1997 by
Robert Hale Limited
London

First Linford Edition
published 1998
by arrangement with
Robert Hale Limited
London

British Library CIP Data

Kirby, Hank J.
    Hellfire Pass.—Large print ed.—
Linford western library
    1. Western stories
    2. Large type books
    I. Title
    823.9'14 [F]

    ISBN 0–7089–5285–2

Published by
F. A. Thorpe (Publishing) Ltd.
Anstey, Leicestershire

Set by Words & Graphics Ltd.
Anstey, Leicestershire
Printed and bound in Great Britain by
T. J. International Ltd., Padstow, Cornwall

This book is printed on acid-free paper

1

Cheyenne

IF Greasy Fallon hadn't made eyes at the pair of young women strolling along the boardwalks of Cheyenne and started a brawl, the trouble at Hellfire Pass might never have happened.

But Fallon, together with several other hands from the Montana-bound trail herd, had a lot of rotgut whiskey under his belt and was in a reckless mood. The Dutch courage made young Greasy Fallon block the path of the two women, bowing low — and staggering at the same time — as he swept off his hat, his lank hair falling forward.

"Ladies! A true, died-in-the-blood Texan at your service — and I mean 'service', you know what I'm sayin'?" He winked and leered and the women

1

straightened, one having the grace to blush deeply, the other going very pale and looking very scared.

Then the two local men appeared out of the barber shop and the big one moved in on Fallon, who was still bowed, grinning up at the women. Hard fingers twisted in the lank hair, yanked him upright, and a big fist hammered down into the middle of Fallon's startled face. One of the women gave a cry as blood spurted from a crushed nose, splashing her skirts, and the other had enough presence of mind to grab her arm and quickly drag her away along the walk as Fallon's pards surged forward.

The big man still had hold of Greasy Fallon who was sagging now, and he flung the semi-conscious man into the trail herders, setting them a'stumbling.

"We ain't got no use for Texans nor no Rebs up here, you sons of bitches. Go on back to your cows an' drive on outta here."

By then his pard had come up alongside, plainly ready to back the big man, and other locals were running across the muddy streets, shouting. Fallon, face bloody, fury burning through the pain he was feeling, now lurched to his feet and launched himself at the big man, butting him in the midriff, arms going about his hips, and ramming him back against the shopfront.

Then it was a melee of crowding bodies and flailing fists, interspersed with shouted curses and crashing glass as a luckless local put his shoulder through the street-front window of the barber's shop. The little barber raged and hurled himself into the brawl, lashing about him with a leather strop indiscriminately.

The fight had spilled over into the street and surged along the walks and muddy gutters down past the druggist's and seemed to settle in front of Holloway's Emporium. Here the men slugged it out toe-to-toe, the trailers yelling for back-up, half-drunken cowboys staggering out of the saloon opposite, charging straight in, slogging away at any face they didn't recognize.

A hitchrail gave way with a splintering crash. Someone ripped up a plank from the boardwalk and waded in swinging. Two men rolled under hitched horses and yelled as the frightened animals stomped on them, whinnying. A man was hurled bodily through a plate glass window of the store and lay amidst glass shards and the display, groaning and bleeding. An awning post was jarred loose and one end of the roof sagged, spilling a few loose shingles into the melee.

By this time most of the town was either involved in or witnessing the riot. And that included the lawmen, the marshal and two deputies pounding up the street from the jailhouse, armed with rifles and shotgun.

The marshal fired one barrel of his Greener over the heads of the brawlers

4

and immediately the fights broke up, only a couple of sly punches thrown after the thunder of the gunshot. Panting, ragged, blood-streaked men swayed and leaned against each other, moaning, sucking popped and split knuckles, squinting out of blood-sticky eyes that were swelling fast, others spitting broken teeth, two men unable to get up off the ground. The ranny who had been thrown through the storefront window lay moaning amidst the broken glass and tumbled display items.

The marshal sounded off, a hard-faced, bitter-mouthed man, no more than five-seven and maybe eighty-five pounds in wet socks, brandishing his shotgun. It was a scathing, telling lecture and insulted the forebears of every man there, but it was plain where his sympathies lay — and they weren't with Texas trail herders.

But he made it short, said he wouldn't throw anyone in jail if the cowboys left town, stayed with their cattle on the holding grounds until the herd was ready to move out.

"I'll go to bat and guarantee that, marshal," said tough, stringbean trail boss, Buckeye Westerman. "Gimme time to get my crew patched up and we'll stay outta your lousy town and hit the Montana trail come sun-up."

"Suits us, Reb!" someone yelled and the marshal scowled.

"You do that, mister. I'm holdin' you responsible. Just one man sneaks back into town an' I'll toss the lot of you in my cells. Now, you folk git, let these Rebs get 'emselves patched up . . . Go on! *Git!* I said!"

The townsfolk, grumbling, dispersed and the eight or nine bleeding and bruised trail men crowded the board-walks.

"Who's gonna pay for my window, marshal?" asked the storekeeper standing beside the shattered display area. He reached in to grab the moaning, bleeding cowboy by the torn shirt. "C'mon, you, get outta there."

A tall, lanky man with long tow hair

6

stepped forward easily and grabbed the storekeeper by the arm, spinning him away from the injured man.

"We take care of our own, mister."

The storeman curled a lip at the southern drawl. "Long as you take care of the cost of a new window."

"Fair enough," said the marshal.

"Now, wait up!" exclaimed Buckeye Westerman. "That's my man lyin' there. He was the one thrown through the glass — you find out who threw him, an' it won't be no trail herder. It was a townsman, so someone from your lousy town pays, mister. Right, marshal?"

The lawman spat. "Goddamn Reb know-it-all. The hell din' you stay down in Dixie? We whopped you once, an' you keep comin' up here we'll damn well do it again."

"That's what I like," commented the tall tow-haired man who was known as Sundance. "Unbiased outlook, forgive and forget . . . You set a good example with your attitude, marshal."

"Shut your mouth, Texan!" the lawman snapped, stabbing a stiffened forefinger at Sundance's face. "You-just-shut-your-mouth!"

Sundance turned away lazily, shouldering the storekeeper out of the way, reaching in to lift out the injured man. Two other cowboys moved in quickly to help. The man was cut in several places, had a lump on his head, but was more dazed than seriously hurt, although some of the cuts would require stitching. Sundance steadied the man and turned to pick up the hat lying amongst the glass shards.

It was then that he saw the silver tray — and, scattered about now, the remainder of the coffee set lying in amongst the debris. Fluted silver coffee pot, sugar bowl, cream jug, a couple of spoons.

They were all lying on crumpled velvet and he guessed the service had been on display in the window before being disturbed by the hurtling body of the cowboy.

His big hands were shaking slightly as he picked up the tray and turned it so that he could read some engraving in the centre of the chased design.

Presented to Colonel Jacob Hammer by his grateful Company 'C' for leading them safely through Hell. Alma, Georgia, 1864.

Then the storekeeper snatched the tray out of Sundance's hand. "I'll take that!"

"Who's this Colonel Hammer?" A couple of cowboys, and Buckeye Westerman, looked sharply at Sundance as he spoke. They had never heard so much tension in his usually lazy voice. His battered face was set hard, his eyes narrowed as he glowered down at the storekeeper. The man was plainly disconcerted by the stare and stepped back, cradling the coffee tray against his chest. Then he ran a tongue around his lips before answering Sundance.

"He ain't no good news to you,

feller. He was with Sherman on the March."

Sundance may have stiffened slightly, unaware that everyone was watching him closely. "Through Georgia?"

The storekeeper smiled crookedly. "Only march I know of that was worthwhile, taught you Johnny Rebs a lesson you'll never forget."

"You're right there," Sundance allowed quietly and the marshal frowned and stepped forward.

"All right. If this is workin' up to more trouble, it can stop right now."

Sundance met and held the tough lawman's gaze. "I just wanted to know about this Hammer, is all." He took the tray up again, turned it over and ran a forefinger along a shallow groove on the underside. It looked years old, almost like a bullet groove, though of a small calibre, say .22. The smoky eyes lifted again to the storekeeper.

"Colonel Hammer live around here then?"

"Right out through Hellfire Pass, one

of the biggest and best spreads in all of Wyoming. Highly respected man is the Colonel — he's a war-hero type, but I wouldn't go botherin' him, I was you. I reckon he ain't got no more reason than the rest of us to like Rebs, mebbe less. But he's a peaceable type. Which don't mean his crew has to be, you savvy?"

"I don't aim to bother him," Sundance said handing back the tray. "Must be well-liked for his men to give him an entire silver coffee service."

"Had a whip-round, I expect. Yeah, everyone likes the Colonel. I'm honoured the set's on permanent display in my store."

Sundance nodded and then the impatient marshal broke it up and the cowboys stumbled away, Buckeye Westerman detailing three, including the man who had been thrown through the store window, to go see a sawbones.

"Rest of you come on back to the herd with me."

Riding out of town towards the

11

holding grounds, Sundance rode his chestnut with the light mane up alongside Buckeye.

"Boss, I'd like to draw my time."

Westerman tripped swiftly in the saddle, thumbed back his hat a little to look squarely at the tall cowboy.

"Drawin' your time? You signed on all the way to Montana, amigo."

"Gone far enough. Too cold for me to go any further north. I'm a Georgia boy, Buckeye. Used to steam heat. Never could abide cold weather, and it's comin' on fall and I heard around town that they've already had light snow up in Montana."

"Man, that's up along the Canadian border! We ain't goin' north of Butte, along the old Bozeman Trail."

Sundance shook his head. "Sorry, Buckeye. I'm pulling out. You ain't got the cash to pay me off, send it to me, care of General Delivery, El Pueblo, Big Bend, Texas."

They rode in silence for a spell, the other sick and sorry cowboys

12

concentrating on staying in their saddles.

"Somethin' to do with that Colonel?" asked Buckeye suddenly and Sundance looked at him squarely, not speaking. "You seemed to know there'd be a gouge in the base of that tray, Sundance."

After a hesitation, Sundance nodded. "Yeah. I put it there with my first rifle, a .22, when I was eleven years old." He held up a hand quickly as Buckeye Westerman started to ask the inevitable follow-up question. "Leave it at that, Buckeye."

The trail boss continued to scrutinize him for a short time, then nodded. "I'll have your money by supper time — Sundance, you're a good hand and I'll miss you on this drive. If you need help before we pull out . . . ?"

Sundance shook his head. "No, thanks, Buckeye. What I need is some warm clothes . . . "

"Oh? Figurin' on stayin' a spell then, not hightailin' it back to warmer range?"

Sundance's wide thin lips twitched in a faint smile. "Mebbe I can stand it a little longer — till I'm finished up here."

Westerman nodded slowly. "Remember what I said — if you're still here by the time we come back, you watch out for us and we'll ride to Texas together."

"Just might do that — if I'm still around."

They made the rest of the ride in silence and an hour after he collected his pay due to him, Sundance pulled out, slipping away into the early northern night, making no more sound than a ghost.

He had arrived alone, way back in Matagorda, Texas, and now he had left the same way. No explanations. No farewells.

A true loner.

Riding into hell, his brain storming with a rage he thought he had left behind him in his fire-blackened home state of Georgia almost ten years ago.

2

The Pass

HE stopped in Cheyenne to buy some warm clothing, a corduroy hip-length jacket with a quilted lining that could be removed by undoing a series of buttons, two flannel shirts and a new set of long-handled underwear. The store he chose was not the one that had displayed the silver coffee set, but another in the next block, smaller and more businesslike. The man behind the counter recognized him in the dim light of the oil lamps, he was sure, but he was civil enough and didn't appear to overcharge just because he was a trail herder, and a southerner.

He purchased two cartons of .44 rimfire cartridges for his new break-action Smith and Wesson pistol and the battered old Winchester '66 rifle, and some grub staples. As the man toted it all up and made change he said quietly, "Wouldn't plan on stayin' over in town, I was you, cowboy." At Sundance's quizzical look, he added, "Marshal Monroe can be mean. He sure don't like anyone goin' agin his orders. I heard he told that Buckeye feller he'd hold him responsible if just one of his men came back into town . . ."

"I quit. I'm pulling out for someplace warmer."

The storekeeper arched his eyebrows. He glanced at the packages. "That's cold-weather clothin'."

Sundance said nothing as he gathered his packages, nodded, started to turn away and then swung back.

"How come this Colonel Hammer keeps that silver coffee set displayed in Holloway's store?"

"It's Hammer's store, really. Bought Holloway out after the war, just kept the name. I dunno who suggested he keep that silver tray on permanent display in the window, but he went along with the idea. Always figured it was kinda strange. I mean, if his men thought so much of him, why don't he keep the thing out at his ranch on the mantelpiece . . . ?"

Sundance nodded. "Was thinking along the same lines. And thanks. You're the first person in this town not to remind me I'm a Reb and not any too welcome."

The man grinned, showing yellowed, worn teeth. "I welcome anyone who pays cash . . . but this is a Reb-hatin' town. Too many of you trail herders come through and leave a shambles behind you. That's why, I guess."

Sundance asked directions to Hellfire Pass and the storekeeper snapped up his head but told him to ride northwest, keeping north of the Laramie trail.

"Pass'll bring you out to the Rock River — and Colonel Hammer's spread." He finished with a quizzical lift to his

17

voice but Sundance merely thanked him and left.

He stopped at the feed-and-grain store, bought a sack of oats for the chestnut, then rode on out of night-time Cheyenne, pulling his new corduroy jacket tightly across his chest.

* * *

It was the longest and narrowest pass Sundance had ever seen, stretching for five miles, pinched in the middle like a ribbon about to be tied in a bow. Fact was, both ends even curved out like the wings of a bow, sandy-floored canyons really, the actual pass only that nipped-in section, but locals called the whole kit-and-caboodle Hellfire Pass.

It was named after a battle with a mixed band of Indians, Arapahoe, Sioux, Lakota, Cheyenne, even a few Nez Perces. Under the leadership of Red Hand, a bloody-minded renegade Oglalla, they figured to take and hold the pass and prevent white settlers from moving into traditional lands. But the cannon and Gatling and Hotchkiss guns of the Seventh Cavalry had massacred the fanatical warriors, although the soldiers paid dearly first. Custer had named it Massacre Canyon but someone in the Cartographic Office in Washington had inked in the name Hellfire Pass and it had stuck, being just as appropriate as Custer's name for it.

Sundance knew all this vaguely, information he had picked up over trailside campfires, when men talked over coffee and cigarettes before turning in. There was always gossip at such places, but he had found it easy enough to sort out the real information that might one day be useful from the exaggerated tales most drifters told. He had done his own share when he had been coaxed into contributing to the circle around the campfire, often by way of payment for a meal, giving company and news in exchange for the food. That was the way of the lonely trail, peopled by lonely men, glad of another human being's company even if only for an hour or so.

Not that company or lack of it ever bothered the man known as Sundance: in truth, he preferred to be alone. Had done for nigh on ten years now, ever since he had left his youth behind one bloody and fiery night back at Keystone.

The early sun had not yet penetrated into Hellfire Pass and Sundance built up his campfire amongst the rocks to ward off the chill, poured another cup of coffee and wrapped his hands around the battered tin mug while he sipped slowly.

He had no plan. It had all happened so quickly and the decision to quit had risen out of some depths of his mind on the ride back to the holding ground, catching him a little off-guard as he heard himself telling Buckeye Westerman he wanted to draw his time.

Well, he'd done it and here he was

and somewhere at the other end of this pass was Hammer's land. He had skirted several small homesteads along the river before the rise up to this pass, seeing them indistinctly in the grey pre-dawn light, but gaining a sense of the rich soil within the fenced acres. They made a kind of ragged patchwork from what he had seen, crops ready for harvest before the weather became too cold, likely the womenfolk already working at preserves, bottling their fruit and vegetables to see them through the long winters they had in this part of the country.

Rich farming land along the river bottoms, giving way to this arid-looking canyon which in turn narrowed down to the pass through the Storm Creek Range. He guessed that wide ribbon of water that he thought of as a river was Storm Creek.

He was just getting the lay of the land in his head, knowing it could mean survival. So when he broke camp, he rode around the canyon, inspecting its walls and overhangs and wind-scoured caves, put the chestnut back out towards the homesteads and climbed a'ways up the slopes of the range. He hadn't spent much time in the army, but Fiddler, the old veteran guard at Andersonville, had given him a lot of good advice that he had been forced to put into practice more than once since. It had saved his neck, and he had never forgotten that grit-tough old soldier's words:

"Preparation, son. That's what wins battles. Git the lay of the land you aim to fight over, study it, mark well your escape routes, never let yourself be worked into a corner — always make sure you got at least one door outta wherever you be — that way, even if you don't win, you got a chance of comin' back another day for another crack at it."

There was more — detailed ways of living off the land in enemy territory, silent ways of killing a man, brutal ways — Fiddler had lived with the

Comanche for years, boasted he had three Indian wives in their territory, and two white ones in Tennessee. He was scarred and scrawny and his breath stank and he wheezed like a leaky steam pipe, but he was well into his sixties and said he aimed to see his eighties and die at the end of a rope, executed for rape.

But a Yankee bullet had been the one thing Fiddler hadn't been able to plan against.

Shaking his thoughts of the past, Sundance swung back into the southern canyon end of Hellfire Pass and rode on through the narrow, twisting length, the rugged walls at last warming under the slanting rays of the sun.

The trail was well-worn and he saw plenty of signs where cattle and horses had been driven through, likely on the way to the railhead at Cheyenne or swinging to Laramie and the military markets. He hadn't asked how big Hammer's land was but he had somehow gotten the impression that it was a large spread. Why not? There was plenty of open range available for the taking in Wyoming. Parts of it reminded him of Texas, except for the weather which was too changeable for his liking. This was his first visit to Wyoming. When the herd had started out from Matagorda on the Texas coast, the destination had been Oglalla, Nebraska, but the buyer there had insisted that part of the deal be that the herd was delivered to a newly-formed Ranchers' Alliance outside of Butte, Montana.

Leery of the cold weather approaching, Sundance had allowed himself to be talked into signing on for the new drive with Buckeye Westerman, taking the trail boss's word that they would be in and out by early fall.

Only thing was, he was thinking of fall as it was down south, hadn't realized that the season this far north was almost equivalent to a southern winter. Well, not quite, but way too cold for him.

Mind, if there hadn't been that incident with the silver tray in Cheyenne, he would have stayed with the herd. His own father had always drummed into him that when he gave his word, a man should stand by it and only truly exceptional circumstances would be excuse enough for him to go back on it.

This was 'exceptional' enough, he figured . . .

He had really acted without much thought. It had happened, and next instant he knew exactly what he had to do. Just *how* he was going to accomplish it he hadn't yet worked out, but that would come after he found . . .

He reined in abruptly, coming out of the narrow pass into the northern canyon, seeing the dust and now hearing the commotion halfway down the western wall. The pall of dust boiled and swirled and he glimpsed boulders and what looked like a mustang throwing a fit. Then he saw the rider.

Only he wasn't riding any more. He had fallen out of the saddle and his boot was caught in the stirrup and now he was being dragged by the frantic horse. Something had spooked the bronc badly and it was jumping with all four feet stiffened, coming down right alongside the rider, maybe occasionally hitting him, although he didn't hear any human cries. Likely the man was already unconscious, his body slewing and bouncing, cannoning off rocks.

Judas priest, he would be lucky if he was still alive.

Sundance was already spurring in, taking in the scene and its potential disaster for the downed rider as he closed on the wildly bucking sorrel. Its eyes were white and wide and rolling, nostrils flared and snorting, and he glimpsed something moving between the rocks and knew what was wrong.

The horse had either been bitten by the snake or spooked by it. More likely bitten the way it was behaving.

Sundance rode in fast, leaning out of the saddle as the chestnut closed, Bowie knife in hand. The rider was lost in a pall of dust, arms flopping, clothes torn, as he slashed at the stirrup leather. The blade was honed like a razor, severed the leather easily and the rider dropped away.

But the sorrel, mad with pain or the snake's venom, tried to bite the chestnut, rammed a shoulder against him and almost unseated Sundance as he was straightening.

He gripped hard with his knees and without hesitation drew his Smith and Wesson and put a shot through the sorrel's brain, hauling the chestnut back fast as the animal reared one final time and then crashed over on its side, missing the downed rider by less than a yard . . .

Sundance quit saddle in a hurry, smoking pistol still in one hand, the Bowie blade in the other. He looked for the snake but it had gone now, and he holstered both weapons, turned to the injured rider lying face down in the sand. He stopped, frowning, staring down at the torn denim trousers and the askew leather shotgun chaps, one small boot with a heel torn off. The shirt was torn, too, exposing an expanse of smooth white flesh — and dark brown hair spilled to the shoulders, half hiding the face, from beneath a narrow-brimmed hat.

He knew before he turned the body over that it was a girl and when the ripped shirt fell free at the front, he was not surprised to see two small perfect breasts exposed, their roundness marred by fresh rash-like patches where she had been dragged over the sand. He pushed back the hair gently, saw her face was banged up some but nothing that would leave any permanent scars. Which would have been a shame, if she had been scarred, for it was a beautiful face, tanned, oval, smooth with the taut unmarked skin of youth. He lifted one eyelid and saw the eye was brown, the pupil a little dilated.

He sat back on his haunches, thumbing back his hat. Then he reached out and pulled the shirt closed over her breasts, holding it in place with the single button that hadn't been torn off. He brought his canteen, punched in the top of his hat and poured some water into it. He took some old rags from his saddlebags and began to bathe her face, washing away the dirt and smears of blood, dabbing at a bead of blood at the corner of full lips, feeling an urge to kiss them briefly before he cussed himself for a fool and got on with the job of tending to her.

This was a beautiful young woman, maybe eighteen or nineteen, he figured, though he wasn't very experienced at guessing women's ages, although she looked about the same age as Cassie had been before she . . .

He turned quickly at the sounds of hoofs, just as he opened the girl's shirtfront again and started to bathe the gravel-rash on her breasts. She rolled her head once, making a small noise, and he figured the water must have stung.

One hand was resting on her breast as he watched four riders come thundering into the canyon from the north, all wearing leather chaps and work clothes that labelled them as cowboys. There was a young man leading, a solid-looking hombre in his early twenties, a few years younger than Sundance. He skidded his dusty zebra dun to a halt, leapt from the saddle as Sundance started to stand. But the young rider didn't slow down even when one of the other three called sharply, "Morg!"

Sundance was still off-balance when the man hit him full force. He staggered, trying not to stand on the unconscious girl, but his feet tangled with her legs and as he started to go down, Morg hit him on the jaw.

Sundance fell onto the dead horse, rolled away as the young hellion kicked at his head. Temper rising now, Sundance caught the boot, twisted savagely, and put Morg down in the dust. The man was quick, rolled and bounced back to his feet and came in swinging as Sundance straightened. The older rider who had called out earlier was shouting something now but Sundance couldn't make out what it was. He ducked under Morg's swing, planted a blow in the man's midriff.

The young cowpoke gagged and stopped dead, doubling over. Sundance hit him on the jaw, kicked his legs out from under him. *Damn!* Morg bounced up, still gasping for breath, but game as they come, fists swinging. One blow took Sundance on the temple and for a few seconds it was Fourth of July, and then, as his vision cleared, he was hammered back against a boulder by a barrage of blows that left him breathless and sick. He sagged there and Morg, blood running from his nostrils, stepped in and aimed a brutal kick at his midriff, driving the stiffened leg forward as if he would impale Sundance on the high heel.

Sundance flung himself to one side

and Morg grunted as his boot drove into the unyielding rock sending pain up his leg into his hip and pelvic area. He stumbled, fighting to keep balance.

Sundance, mighty mad now, stepped in and smashed blow after blow into the man, flinging him against a boulder, pinning him there by the shoulder with his left hand, hammering his right into the bloody face again and again — until strong hands grabbed him and twisted his arms behind his back and the older rider, who had been doing the yelling, stepped between him and Morg and set his boots and hooked two savage blows into Sundance's midriff.

He gagged and his legs buckled but the two men held him from falling and the older ranny backhanded him across the face, saying, "Let him go."

The other men released their holds and Sundance fell to his knees, slowly bending forward until his forehead touched the sand, hugging his midriff, fighting for breath. A boot drove into his ribs and sent him skidding onto his side. When he could see, he saw the older rider holding Morg back, the young cowboy's blood-streaked face murderous as he struggled to get at Sundance and stomp him again.

He was flung brutally back against a boulder and Morg grunted as the older man held him there.

"Stay *put*, damn you, Morg! Let's get the straight of this before you kill him, goddamnit! *Look*, look around you — can't you see what's happened? Rachel's been — thrown and dragged and this feller's cut her free. Look at her boot still jammed in that stirrup and the cut strap . . . Christ, man, when're you gonna quit goin' off half-cocked?"

"You see where his hand was, Gabe?" panted Morg, still fighting to get past the other man so as to reach Sundance who was sitting up now, rubbing his mid-section.

"You move and so help me I'll

rope you to that rock!" snapped Gabe, shoving Morg roughly. "Now, simmer down . . . " He turned to Sundance and offered a hand.

Sundance slapped it aside, climbed slowly to his feet without assistance, eyes hard and still burning with anger as he glared at Morg.

"Now *you* simmer down, too, mister! This was a mistake, is all."

"Yeah — and he made it," Sundance said, taking a step towards Morg who immediately put up his fists.

Gabe shoved Sundance away, drew his six-gun, a heavy old cap-and-ball Dragoon, and punched a bullet into the sand between the two men.

"Now that's it! Next one makes a move to continue the fight gets his foot mangled." He thumbed back the hammer, the heavy barrel wavering between the men. Both remained where they were, silent. Gabe looked at Sundance. "Mister, we're grateful for what you done for young Rachel, and you'll have to excuse Morg's hotheadedness, bein' her older brother an' so havin' the notion he has to look out for her — I seen where your hand was, but I also seen the cloth. It's obvious she's injured there." He stopped as Morg moved suddenly to his sister and knelt, closing the shirt over her scarred breasts. He shot a murderous look at Sundance.

"He din' have to do that. Touch her there . . . "

"Mebbe not, but I'd say he was just cleanin' her up in general! Mister, you kinda spoiled things for yourself some."

Sundance waited, dabbing at cuts on his face, mopping blood from his lips.

"Yeah! — you just done got yourself some credit with the Colonel, savin' his daughter like you done, but you earned a heap of demerits, too, by beatin' up on his son thataway."

Sundance stiffened. "Colonel?"

"Yeah. Colonel Jacob Hammer — these

are his kids. Rachel's the better-lookin' one."

Gabe smiled crookedly but Morgan Hammer scowled, unamused. He still looked like he wanted to kill Sundance.

3

Medicine Basin

GABE SPOONER told Sundance that he and the others were driving a small herd from Colonel Hammer's ranch into Cheyenne. Rachel had ridden on ahead, anxious to do some shopping in town and pick up some clothes she had ordered.

Apparently a rattler had struck her horse — they found the snakebite on the left foreleg — and it had gone crazy, catching her off-guard. When it had thrown her, her small foot had slipped through the stirrup and caught there. No doubt she would have been stomped to death if Sundance hadn't happened along. His gun shot when he had put her horse out of its misery had been heard by a point rider and that was how the group had come thundering through the pass and seen him tending the injured girl.

Spooner was Hammer's foreman and had worked for him for many years. While he stood with Sundance, he set Morgan and the other two hands to building a *travois* for carrying Rachel back to the ranch.

"You'd better come along, Sundance — Colonel'll want to thank you."

"I'm not looking for thanks." But Sundance was pleased at the invitation: it solved one problem, how he was going to get close to Hammer. A little reluctance wouldn't go astray he figured, as long as he didn't overdo it. "I'm glad I was on hand to help out."

The girl was still out of it, pale and battered, when they gently loaded her onto the *travois*. Morgan straightened and glared at Sundance. There was no give in the man. He had refused to shake hands and made no effort to disguise his hatred for southerners. Sundance wondered about that because the man would have been far too young to have been in the war. Sundance figured he was no more than twenty-two.

Maybe he inherited his hatred from the Colonel.

"No, you gotta come meet the Colonel," Gabe Spooner insisted. "Judas, he'd kick my butt if I let you go without him havin' a chance to thank you."

Sundance nodded, but still seemed reluctant. "Look, Gabe, I can't change my accent. From what I've seen of things, Rebs ain't welcome up here."

"You mean Yankees are down in Texas?"

Sundance smiled thinly, scratching at his head, running his fingers through his long, sweat-matted hair.

"Well — guess you're right. Works both ways — OK, I'll come meet your Colonel."

Morg growled deep in his throat and spat on the ground but said nothing as they mounted and moved out, the *travois* being pulled by Gabe Spooner's blue dun.

"You're a long way from home," the old foreman said with a query in his voice as they rode through the narrow, twisting pass.

Sundance told him about coming north with the trail herd, but added a lie: "Like the look of this country. Figured to check it out some . . . understand there's land up for grabs somewhere around here, too."

Gabe, glancing back to make sure the girl was all right, curled a lip under his tobacco-stained moustache.

"Homestead land. Back there along the river bottoms, you must've seen it . . . You don't strike me as a nester-type Sundance."

Sundance shrugged. "If I had some land, even a quarter-section, I'd run me a few beeves. I've farmed before, grew up on one, matter of fact, only got into cowboying after the war."

Gabe stared hard at him for a moment before nodding. "Well, if you want to ranch, through the pass out on the prairie's the place. Beyond the Colonel's there's free range, if you've a notion to try your hand at it — takes some money to get started, though."

There was another query in his words there.

"Yeah, well, I'd have to prove up, I guess. But I dunno if I could take the cold. Figured I'd see what was on offer, stick around working at something until I see how much colder it gets before I commit myself to homesteading."

"Man, you're a baby if you figure this is cold!" said Morgan Hammer, riding on Sundance's left. The tow-haired man glanced at him.

"I was talking to Gabe, but since you mention it, Morg, I am something of a babe when it comes to real cold. I was born mid-summer in Georgia and that made my blood thin. Can't take the bitter cold and if it gets real bad up here, I'll be heading south again quick as I can."

Gabe laughed shortly to break the

41

tension, but said, his smile kind of taut, "Georgia? I thought you was from Texas?"

"Moved there when I was young," Sundance said shortly and then they came up with the rest of the herd and Gabe gave his orders to the cowboys and Morg, while he and Sundance continued on up the huge valley, the girl beginning to moan a little in the *travois*.

Morgan wasn't any too pleased that he was ordered to take the herd on into Cheyenne but Gabe had insisted and he had obeyed with bad grace.

"Got a chip on his shoulder, has Morg," opined Sundance. "Any reason for him hating southerners?"

"Dunno," Gabe said shortly. "Seems to have been born with it — look, when we top that ridge yonder, you'll see the Colonel's place. Calls it the J-Link-H." Sundance had seen the brand on some of the cattle, the J acting as the front upright of the H.

He felt his breath catch when they

topped the rise and looked out over an immense basin with a big cluster of ranch buildings almost in the centre.

"That's only part of it, what you can see — stretches back across the Rock River and up into the Medicine Bow range. Biggest spread in the north and that includes them British holdin's up in Montana."

The basin was locked in by ranges and although Sundance stood in the stirrups, he couldn't make out any passes through them. He commented on this and Gabe nodded soberly.

"The one big drawback. Hellfire Pass is the only way in or out of Medicine Basin . . . but it's a real short-cut to Cheyenne. Without it, the Colonel'd have to drive his cows way round over the Medicine Bows — there's some low foothills that could be crossed without too much trouble."

"Wouldn't have much beef left on 'em if he had to do that."

"Yeah — but we've got Hellfire Pass so it's not an issue. C'mon, we'd better get down there. Rachel's stirring and she must need attention."

They heeled their mounts forward.

★ ★ ★

Sundance was waiting on the wide veranda that ran across the front of the big, two-storeyed log ranch house, smoking contentedly. He felt at his ease, boots up on the rails, leaning back in a ladderback chair. While the ranch womenfolk had tended to Rachel and Gabe had brought the Colonel up to date, Sundance had taken a hot bath and dressed in his new underwear and shirt and felt way better — and warmer.

The doctor arrived from Cheyenne, having been sent by the man Gabe had told to ride on ahead of the herd. He was young and flustered and had ridden his horse hard.

"Where's Miss Hammer?" he panted at Sundance and the Reb had jerked a thumb towards the front door and the doctor had disappeared through it with his black bag.

Minutes later, Colonel Hammer came out, offering his right hand as Sundance got lazily to his feet.

"I'm very much obliged, sir, for what you did for my daughter."

The Colonel was a ramrod straight man, shorter than Sundance's six-feet-one only by an inch or so. His hair was long and peppered with silver, and he sported a Van Dyke beard and moustache. His face was deeply tanned, deep cut with lines around the mouth and the corners of the piercing blue eyes. He walked with a slight limp and Sundance was to notice later that it came and went, according to the company.

He shook briefly with the Colonel and tried to act as casual as he was trying to appear although his belly was knotted up inside as he faced this man.

"Sundance — some kind of Texan name, I suppose?"

"It's an Indian dance, Colonel. I spent a little time hunting with the Comanche and later, on my first trail drive, I got a little drunk and did a war dance on a saloon bar. It started a fracas and someone named me 'Sundance' afterwards. It kinda stuck."

"You'll have to be careful you don't forget your real name," the Colonel said carefully and the penetrating blue eyes asked a question which Sundance chose to ignore.

"Sundance is as good as any down where I've been working these past ten years."

They sat down and Hammer offered Sundance a cigar, which he accepted. They lit up and then an Indian woman servant brought a tray with a decanter of whiskey and two glasses. She poured liquor into the glasses and went back into the house, leaving the tray. The Colonel handed Sundance one glass, picked up the other.

"Again, my thanks, sir, for what you

did for Rachel. There's no doubt you saved her life."

"Lucky I was on the spot, is all . . . this is fine whiskey, Colonel."

Hammer smiled. "Some of your southern bourbon. Got a taste for it during the war."

"During your march through Georgia with Sherman?"

Hammer's face closed and his eyes took on the appearance of blue chips of ice. "You say that with a certain latent hostility, Sundance. Of course, Gabe told me your home state is Georgia."

The words trailed off and Sundance remained silent. Hammer frowned a little.

"War is a terrible thing, Sundance. We all had to do things that will haunt us for the rest of our lives."

"The burning of Georgia was an atrocity. Sherman should've been brought to account for that."

"Sundance, Sherman did what he had to to win the war. We all did — but

47

it's over now. Shall we leave it?"

Sundance smiled thinly. "I'm sorry, Colonel. You're right of course, and I was out of line to speak the way I did while your guest."

"The old southern code of manners, eh? Well, we'll change the subject, that ought to do it . . . how would you like to work for me?"

"You don't have to offer me a job just because I . . . "

"My motives aren't important, Sundance. Would you like to work for me?"

"Doing what?"

"Ranch work — I'll give you two weeks to prove to me whether I should make you a top hand or just keep you on a lowly cowpoke's wages — you'll have a warm berth through winter."

Sundance smiled. "I dunno — I'm beginning to think I won't be able to see out a winter up here."

The Colonel spread his hands. "That's up to you. I won't hold you to anything. You leave when you feel like it — job's there if you want it. I like to square my debts."

Sundance hesitated only briefly. "Reckon I'd be loco not to take your offer, Colonel. Obliged to you . . . "

Hammer nodded, sipped his drink. "Gabe mentioned you might be looking for homestead land."

Sundance shrugged. "It was a notion I had, but, like I said, I figure it's gonna be too cold for me. I'll be glad of work while I look around and see what the weather's going to do, though."

"Well, I won't mislead you. Winters up here will freeze the piss in your bladder, but you get used to them. We're originally from Wisconsin so we have a touch of snow in the blood — you've no idea how I suffered in that humid heat down in your native State during the war."

As casually as he could Sundance asked, "What part of Georgia were you in, Colonel?"

"All over the southern part mostly . . . "

"Oh, sure, I saw on that silver tray

in Cheyenne where it was presented to you for an action at Alma."

The blue eyes flickered. "You know Alma?"

"I was born near there."

"Is that so? Very pretty country."

"Too bad it had to burn."

"Seems we're back to the war again, Sundance . . . "

"Sorry. I lost family and friends during Sherman's March-To-The-Sea — hard to forget."

The Colonel heaved to his feet, rolling the empty glass between his fingers. "I'll send Gabe out to show you where to bunk and so on . . . " He thrust out his hand abruptly. "And my thanks again for what you did for Rachel. She's very, very dear to me."

"To Morg, too, I think."

Colonel Hammer laughed shortly. "Bit of a hothead, Morg. Takes after his old man — but he'll come round." Then the face straightened and the voice took on a steely edge and Sundance knew this man's troops would have been highly disciplined. "He's a good fighter, is Morg. But I wouldn't want you two to butt heads again — you understand?"

"Won't be my doing if we do, Colonel."

"You don't — quite — understand what I'm saying. I mean, don't — *ever* — fight Morg again, no matter what the circumstances, or how many punches he throws your way. *Now* do you understand?"

Sundance held that icy stare levelly, his grey eyes clouding. "I always hit back, Colonel. Maybe not right away but — always. Sometime."

Hammer checked himself as he started to retort angrily, clapped a hand on Sundance's shoulder. "Well, let's leave things there — This homesteading — I'm interested in some land out along the river. If I can buy it — maybe if *you* could buy it in my name, with my money, of course, we might be able to come to some arrangement where you work it for me . . . think about

51

it. Could have possibilities."

The man walked away, leaving Sundance standing there, mighty puzzled.

★ ★ ★

Standing outside the bunkhouse after stowing his warbag in an empty upper bunk, Sundance thumbed back his hat and looked at the three large corrals, the big solid barn and the blacksmith's forge.

"You build to last up here," he opined to Gabe Spooner.

"Got to, the weather we get." The foreman studied his rugged face. "Hear the Colonel told you to steer clear of Morg. You'd do well to heed him. Everyone walks wide around Morg."

"Didn't notice you walking too wide at the pass."

"I got me a few privileges."

"Where's Mrs Hammer?"

"Don't go askin' — all you need to know is she ain't comin' back."

"Funny way of sayin' she's dead."

"Did I say that?"

"No-ooo, guess not. OK. I'm not all that interested anyway." Then he saw the Indian woman on the porch gesturing for him to approach. Puzzled, he walked to the foot of the steps.

"Miss Rachel — you come."

"Is it OK for me to come into the house?"

"Miss Rachel say you come."

Sundance shrugged and followed the Indian woman inside and up the stairs and down a short dim hall. She opened the door of the end room and stood aside for him to enter.

Sundance went in with his hat in his hand, immediately uncomfortable in the very feminine room. The girl was sitting up in bed amongst a lot of lace-edged pillows, some frilly nightgown buttoned to her neck. Her hair gleamed with recent brushing and there were smears of iodine and arnica tincture on the bruises and grazes on her face.

She smiled and immediately winced,

touching her swollen jaw, then offered him her small right hand.

"I wanted to thank you in person — Sundance? Or is there a 'mister' goes before the name?"

"Just 'Sundance' ma'am." He walked forward, hearing the door close gently behind him, and took the girl's soft hand in his. He dropped it quickly and she smiled.

"I can see all this female frippery makes you uncomfortable, so I won't keep you — I'm very grateful you came along when you did, and I'm glad you'll be working for Dad. I hope I'll have a chance to show you my appreciation in some more — tangible way."

"No need, ma'am."

"Rachel, please . . . "

"OK — Rachel. But there's no need. I'm just glad you're OK. Nothing permanent, I hope?"

"Bruised ribs, some cuts and abrasions, and the mother of all headaches — the doctor's prescribed medicine and a few days' rest in my bed, but while I'll take the pills and potions, I don't intend to stay a'bed for that long."

"Might be as well to do like the sawbones says, ma'am — Rachel. You took a bad fall."

"We'll see — You can go whenever you want, Sundance."

He nodded, hesitated, then turned and left.

She was smiling, but it faded slowly and she tugged at her lower lip thoughtfully with her teeth before she remembered it was swollen and cut.

She wondered just why Sundance had made her feel so — uneasy . . .

4

Mad Dog

MORGAN HAMMER and his men delivered the small Hammer herd to the cattle agent in Cheyenne and then went to the *Belle of the North* saloon.

He bought drinks for the men — putting it on the Colonel's tab — then went upstairs with one of the painted gals who called herself 'Sherry'.

When he came down, the men had already started back for J-Link-H and that suited him fine. He downed two more whiskies, went out onto the porch and lit up a cheroot, before taking his silver pocket watch out and checking the time. He smiled thinly, feeling the tug at battered flesh as he did so.

For a moment the smile changed to a

scowl as he remembered his brawl with that goddamn Reb, Sundance. But he shook the memory, pushing it to the back of his mind.

His time would come: he would square things, his way.

Right now, he was in too good a mood to dwell on the tow-haired son of a bitch.

He had timed it just right, he figured, when he saw the buckboard with the red-and-yellow lines painted around the seat. He stepped down from the porch, crossed the street, ducked into an alley and came out into a vacant weed-grown lot with a weather-beaten shed in the south corner, leaning a little to one side.

He approached silently, smiling to himself again, coming up on a blank side, easing along the warped clapboards to the door. Suddenly he let out a wild Indian whoop and leapt forward, kicking the door so hard that it broke one hinge. It slammed back against the wall and choking dust fell in clouds from between the planks.

Somewhere in the gloom a woman screamed and Morg laughed, but it was choked back into his throat as something smashed across his shoulders, cannoned off his head, knocking the hat askew, as he staggered into the wall. The plank took him in the midriff and he gagged, fell to one knee, one arm lifted to protect his head.

"Stop! — Judas priest, Kit — it's me!"

The dim shape of the woman stopped the downward swing with the broken plank and then she let it drop, started forward, but checked, hands on her hips. Suddenly she kicked out and her riding boot took him in the side.

"Christ! Ease up, will you?"

"I ought to damn well shoot you, coming in like that! I thought it was a blamed Indian . . . oh, you're just a stupid boy at times, Morgan Hammer, I swear." Then she was helping him to his feet, and kissing him as she held his face between her hands.

"I — guess it was kinda — stupid," he admitted, his hands going first to her waist, and then sliding up under her blouse. She stiffened and he leaned down and kissed her soundly, feeling her hunger, the hunger of the lonely widow.

After a time, she pulled back, flushed and breathless, straightening her clothes, seeing the disappointment on his face. Well, it wouldn't hurt for him to realize that just because he was the Colonel's son didn't entitle him to take any woman he wanted . . .

"What's wrong, Kit?"

"I have to get back. I've been waiting for you too long as it is."

He tried again to caress her and was rebuffed. "But you *did* wait."

"Yes — you look like you've been in a fight."

"Ah, it was nothin'." But he went on to tell her about the incident in the pass. "Lousy Johnny Reb layin' his hand on my sister that way."

"Well, it sounds to me as if he was

only cleaning her up . . . "

"You dunno nothin' about it!" he blazed. "Look, are we going to . . . ? Or not?"

"Not. I told you I have to get back. You're late. And besides, I can smell a whore's cheap perfume on you — Sherry, I suppose?"

"Hey, I had to kill some time. You weren't even in town when the boys were ready to ride out . . . "

"You bastard! You think you can come from a whore straight to me? *No!* Stay away from me, Morg. You're not touching me today — now I'm going. If you want us to meet again, you'd better send me word."

He tried to reach for her but she twisted away and picked up the broken plank again. He jumped back.

"Judas, why'd you bother coming?"

"To meet you — but not half-drunk and reeking of Sherry's cheap perfume . . . "

"Listen," he said, making one last desperate try to hold her here. "I was talking with the old — man he's willing to up his offer. I think I can get you another five hundred."

Kit Dunson stared at him, the dusty sunlight turning her fair hair to a golden halo when she threw down the plank but her words soon wiped the beginning smile off Morgan's battered lips. Truth was known, he was a mite afraid of the older woman. "I sometimes think you're just using me on behalf of the Colonel, Morg. If I find out that's true, I'll kill you — and meantime, you can tell him the answer's still 'no'. I don't want to sell my land on Storm Creek. And nor do any of the other homesteaders. So, if that's the real reason you've been seeing me . . . "

"Hell, no, Kit! What kinda man d'you think I am?"

"I'm not as sure as I thought I was, Morgan . . . but, if you want to see me again, you send word like I said . . . in the usual way."

"Well, just maybe I won't!" he flared

angrily, pouting.

But she slipped out the broken door and was gone. He stood in the doorway and watched her hurry across the weeds and turn down the narrow space between the store and the barber's shop. *Damn woman! Didn't she realize he was doing her a favour?* He swore and suddenly kicked the rotted door savagely, breaking the lower hinge, too. It fell against him and in a rage he slammed it back against the wall of the crumbling shed so hard he tore loose some clapboards. He kicked out several more before he calmed down and, muttering, stormed out across the vacant lot, heading back towards the saloon once he reached Main, ripe for trouble.

★ ★ ★

He downed two more whiskies at the bar and when he growled at the barkeep to put them on his father's tab, the man said, "You're over the limit he allows, Morg. So make this the last one, OK?"

Morg scowled, in an ugly mood, grabbed the barkeep by hooking a finger over his buttoned collar and smashed the man face first onto the bar. The crunch of the man's nose breaking could be heard all through the room. Blood sprayed and the barman slid back in an unconscious heap on the floor behind the bar. The second 'keep rushed to him, looking angrily up at Morg.

"You din' have to do that to Chet! He was only doin' his job."

"You want to try doing your job the way he was?" Morgan asked belligerently and the 'keep shook his head, helping his half-conscious workmate to his feet.

"You help yourself far as I'm concerned. Drink all you want." Under his breath the man added, "Sooner you pass out the better for everyone!"

But Morg merely reached across the bar, took the bottle of whiskey and drank from the neck. He rested his elbows on the bar, raking his wild gaze around the room. Most men lowered their eyes. A couple stared back, but Morg only curled a lip, and turned to the barman as he helped the injured man through the curtained doorway.

"Where's Sherry?"

"Upstairs — and she's busy."

Morg scowled again, took another drink and staggered towards the stairs. He went up by hauling himself by one rail, muttering, paused at the top to suck at the bottle again, before lurching towards the door of Sherry's room.

He heard the bedsprings working and rage surged through him like flame flaring on a match head. He lifted one boot, kicked the door open with a splintering crash and saw the moving couple on the bed.

At the sound of the door smashing into the wall, the customer, startled, rolled away from the semi-naked Sherry.

"What the hell . . . ? Goddamnit,

Hammer, get outta here. I ain't through yet."

"Wrong! You are! Now *you* git!"

"Morg, please!" cried the girl, knowing his rage. Morgan Hammer ignored her, looking at the cowboy, a rugged frontier type who displayed no fear of the young man just because his name was Hammer.

"You going?" Morg demanded impatiently.

"I'll show you who's goin', you son of a bitch!" the cowboy said, lurching to his feet, stumbling against the chair where his trousers lay in a crumpled heap — and where his gunbelt hung over the back.

Morgan's right hand swept up his new Peacemaker from the cut-away holster had had made by the Cheyenne saddler, his finger finding the trigger instantly, thumb cocking the hammer as the barrel cleared leather.

The cowboy's eyes widened and Sherry screamed, cramming her body up against the bedhead as the big gun roared, three times.

The strike of the slugs smashed the cowboy into the wall, jerked him onto his side, where he lay bleeding, already dead.

Morgan blinked through the gunsmoke, staring hard at the dead man, then lifted his gaze to the crying girl.

"You seen it — he went for his gun first!"

"He fell against the chair!"

Morg stepped forward, placed the foresight against her face. "He — went — for — his — *gun*!"

As the first of the curious men from downstairs came thundering down the passage, the frightened whore nodded quickly.

"Yes!" she whispered hoarsely. "He — he went for his gun . . . "

Morgan smiled crookedly, realized he still held the whiskey bottle and took a deep swig as men began crowding into the room.

* * *

Sitting outside the bunkhouse, smoking while he waited for the range crew to come in and have supper, Sundance saw the rider from town arrive and go straight into the big house. Minutes later, the Colonel came out and Gabe yelled at Sundance to saddle the Colonel's horse, the big black with the blaze between the eyes.

By the time he was finishing tightening the cinch, Hammer was beside him, wearing a frock coat over white shirt and striped trousers. Sundance noted he was also wearing a cartridge belt and six-gun. He handed the reins to the man.

"Anything I can do, Colonel?"

Hammer swung into saddle, wrenched the black's head around so sharply that Sundance had to step back quickly. Then the man dug in his silver spurs and rode swiftly out of the yard, heading across the basin towards Hellfire Pass.

Sundance turned as Gabe Spooner came up looking grim. "What was that all about?" he asked the foreman.

"Young Morg. Killed a man in town. Drunk, of course — seems it was a fair enough fight, but it was in a whore's room and that don't set easy with the Colonel. He likes folk to figure his family's above that kinda thing."

"He shouldn't have had Morg then."

Gabe grabbed Sundance's upper arm, steel fingers biting into the muscle. "Quit that. You dunno enough about the Colonel to go makin' remarks like that."

"And you dunno enough about me to know how bad I hate for anyone to grab my gun arm — now turn me loose, Gabe."

Spooner looked startled, but slowly released his hold. He scrubbed a hand around his stubbled jaw, smoothed his moustache. "I ain't sure you're gonna fit in here too well, Sundance."

Sundance shrugged and their eyes locked until Gabe suddenly sighed, thumbed back his hat. "Well, actually you're right. Morg's a hellion, caused the old man all kindsa grief over the years. The Colonel don't approve, but he's mighty strong on family — he'll back 'em all the way to hell and beyond."

Sundance had nothing to say about that.

"First time Morg's killed a man," Gabe added quietly. "Come close a couple times before . . . "

"What ails him?"

Gabe shrugged. "Upbringin' I guess. No mother to rear him, only Indian women or hired governesses. Allowed to run riot pretty much and he's got the Colonel's wild streak in him, which is another reason the Colonel backs him, I guess."

Sundance caught Gabe's eye and asked quietly, "Colonel's wife run out on him? You said Morgan had no mother to rear him and hinted she was still alive earlier . . . "

"I also told you earlier not to ask!"

"I'm just theorizing — like, she left while the kids were young, run off with someone — a southerner, mebbe?"

Gabe Spooner was shaking with anger and his hand dropped to the butt of his big Dragoon. "By Godfrey, you take some chances, Sundance! I got me a bad feelin' about you. I'm beginnin' to regret bringing you back here . . . "

"Was it a southerner?"

"Judas, you damn well push it, don't you? What the hell business is it of yours anyway?"

"I'm from the south and it'd help explain why the Colonel hates Rebs. It sure brushed off on Morg, anyway."

Spooner was silent for a spell, hand still on gun butt. He pursed leathery lips. "Yeah a piece of southern trash. A drummer, for Chrissakes! The Colonel's wife sneakin' off like some whore with a *drummer*."

"Would've been OK if it'd been a Yankee, I guess."

Gabe hit Sundance a backhand blow that brought a trickle of blood to the man's mouth. "You shut up! Where you get off talkin' that way after what the Colonel's offered you?"

"That's twice you've hit me today, Gabe. Don't let there be a third time."

For a moment, he thought the man was about to draw, but the ramrod abruptly turned on his heel and strode away.

★ ★ ★

Morg was surly and very quiet when he rode back into the ranch yard with his father after dark. He was ordered to off-saddle the mounts and turn them into the corrals.

Laughter issued from the bunkhouse and while the Colonel went up to the main house, Morg walked across and stood in the doorway. He grinned when he saw Sundance sprawled amidst the wreckage of the top bunk he had chosen earlier.

Someone had loosened the planks so that when he climbed up, the mattress and supports gave way. Sundance stood

71

slowly, dusting off his clothes. The men waited. "OK boys. You've had your fun. Now let it rest, all right?"

Morg stepped in. "Aw hell, we ain't through with our initiation yet. Seein' as you don't like the cold, maybe we'd better warm your butt for you, huh?"

The room fell silent and the men moved back, leaving Morg and Sundance facing each other.

"Who's gonna do it, you?" Sundance asked quietly.

Morg spread his hands, looking around at the cowboys as if checking for their support. "Why not? I mean, you wanna protest, why you go right ahead."

He half-turned so that Sundance and the others could see the notch carved into the cedar butt of his Peacemaker. He stroked it casually with a thumb nail. He grinned coldly.

"It's gettin' kinda lonely already, Reb!"

Sundance scowled in disgust. "You figure what you did makes you a gunfighter, boy?" Sundance shook his head slowly. "In my book, all it makes you is two-bit scum."

Men dived for cover and Gabe Spooner shouted Morg's name urgently from the doorway as Hammer reached for his Peacemaker with a curse.

Sundance took a long step forward, his Smith and Wesson coming smoothly out of leather, and he laid the weapon brutally across the side of Morg's head.

The man's feet left the ground and he fell unconscious. Through the deathly silence, Sundance's smoky gaze met the bleak eyes of Gabe Spooner.

"Guess that means I'm all through before I even get started, eh?"

Spooner's face was mighty grim. "Damn right! The Colonel won't have you here after this. You blamed fool. You coulda had a future here . . . you git, pronto, mister."

Sundance moved his thumb to the pistol's hammer spur. "You saw what happened. Morg's a mad dog. Mebbe

I'll regret not putting a bullet in him . . . but that's for later. Right now, shuck your guns, gents, and someone saddle my bronc. Quick!"

When he was astride his horse, still covering the men with his sixgun, Sundance looked down at Gabe.

"Tell the Colonel we'll meet again — and ask him if he's ever heard of a place in Georgia called Keystone Plantation — it's where that silver coffee set was stolen from during the war. Just ask him, see what his reaction is."

He swung his mount's head and spurred away, still carrying the image of Gabe Spooner's shocked face, drained of all blood, with him as he headed for Hellfire Pass.

5

Storm Creek Woman

"KEYSTROKE?" exclaimed the Colonel, the hard, cold gaze boring into his foreman. "Who the hell is he, Gabe? He can't be the kid — he was dead wasn't he?"

"They were all dead far as I knew, Colonel . . . but he knows that silver coffee set came from the plantation. He's got some connection to it."

Hammer took a turn around his mahogany desk in his ranch office, stopped by a glass-fronted book case. "Morg all right?"

Gabe nodded. "He will be. He asked for it, Colonel, but I knew we couldn't keep Sundance around after he slugged the boy."

The Colonel nodded, seeming a little distracted. "Be hard to hold him now he's killed a man. Had hell's own job with the damn marshal, too — Gabe, get some men and go after Sundance. Bring him back here — we've got to get to the bottom of this. You shouldn't've let the son of a bitch go . . . "

"Sorry, Colonel. Just thought it best to get him off . . . "

"I'm riding along," a voice cut in curtly.

Both men snapped their heads up as the door opened and Morgan Hammer stood there, a fresh strip of torn rag tied round his head. His eyes were wild and out of focus. "I want that son of bitch, Pa. He's mine . . . "

"You get to bed and stay there."

"No! I've a right to ride along."

The Colonel strode across the room and Gabe winced at the sound of his flat palm cracking across the kid's face. Morgan's head turned on his shoulders and he took a step backwards, startled more than hurt, blinking, his hand trembling as he put it to the reddening mark on his face.

"You've caused the Hammer family enough trouble this day. You do like I say, boy. Get to bed and rest — we'll handle Sundance."

Morgan swallowed, the daze going out of his eyes. They began to pinch down, flaring with building anger.

"*I'm* the one he slugged! I want to kill him!"

"Damn you, boy. Get this killing business out of your head — you were damn lucky tonight, that's all. The marshal wanted to lock you up until he made a thorough investigation. I headed him off but next time you'll end up in jail. I paid off that whore, too, so she'll continue to back your story, but right now — you — do — like — I — say and — *get to bed*!"

It wasn't often that the colonel raised his voice to Morgan and the young man's face straightened abruptly. He knew he had pushed his father about as far as he could this day. Surlily, he nodded, hung his head, lower lip thrust in a characteristic pout, turned and walked slowly towards the stairs leading to the upper floor of the ranch house.

Hammer watched him through the open door as he started to climb slowly, then swung his gaze back to Gabe.

"Best get after Sundance, Gabe. You can rough him up if there's a need, but bring him back to me alive. I need to know who he is and what he knows about Keystone."

"Leave it to me, Colonel. We'll be back in a couple of hours with him . . . draggin' at the end of a rope."

"As long as he can talk when he gets here."

Gabe was already on his way out. Hammer closed the door of his office, went to the sideboy and poured himself a hefty slug of whiskey from a European crystal decanter.

The neck rang against the rim of the glass as his hand trembled uncontrollably.

Sundance crossed the western canyon and entered the narrow cut of Hellfire Pass. It was darker here, the moonlight throwing the shadows of the high walls completely across the pass, making it a black slash at the tip of the canyon.

His horse's hoofs had echoed riding across the canyon and maybe that was why he hadn't heard the pursuers coming fast. But once he reached the entrance to the pass itself his chestnut was walking on sand and he paused, sitting very still so that he didn't even have the slight creak of saddle leather to distract him.

That sounded like riders coming up behind him. At a fast clip, too. *Several* riders. The only place they could be coming from was the J-Link-H — and more than likely they weren't friendly.

None of them had been sorry to see him pull out. He was a Reb, and if he had stayed he would've been the butt of many a 'joke' and he knew he wouldn't have come out unscathed. The rousting might have started out as fun but it would have escalated as the time went by until they got the reaction they wanted from him — but Morgan had precipitated that.

As soon as he had slugged the mean kid he knew he would have to leave. That was OK — at the time he thought it was a good chance to throw that question about Keystone at Gabe. He would have liked to have seen the Colonel's reaction, but those riders were likely part of it.

Hammer had sent them after him, whether to kill him or drag him back more dead than alive, he didn't know.

But he aimed to find out.

They would overhaul him before he could get through the pass. They knew this area better than their own names. There would be short cuts across that canyon that would bring them well within rifle shot of him before he had gone more than a few yards into the pass.

So, it was time to hole up. Wait for them, and talk to them over the sights of a cocked rifle. He would have all the advantage, being in the darkness of the pass, unseen, while they were out there in the canyon in the full light of the moon . . .

He ground-hitched the chestnut behind a jutting rock, slid the Winchester from the scabbard and took a part-carton of spare cartridges from his saddlebag. Patting the horse and speaking softly to it, he started up the slope which quickly steepened into the wall itself, slid the rifle barrel through his belt at the back, shoved the spare ammunition inside his jacket and began to climb.

Ten feet seemed to be far enough. He had dark rock behind him and in front, the latter only coming to waist level. He could see the spread of the moonlit canyon through the end of the pass and the first rider, only a dark shape right now, but coming in fast enough.

Sundance slid his rifle free, took out the spare carton of ammo and tore off the cover. He set it on a flat section of rock, thumbed back his hat a little and snugged the rifle butt against his shoulder. By the time he had sighted along the rifle, three more riders had appeared behind the first, a man he figured looked mighty like Gabe Spooner.

The oldster held up a hand, hauling rein, the other three skidding their mounts, obviously not prepared for the halt.

"The hell, Gabe?" snapped one man and Sundance recognized the voice as that of a hawkfaced ranny they called Mitch O'Reilly.

"Don't you have enough sense not to go ridin' into a dark area like that without checkin' it out first?" snapped Gabe, rifle in hand, the old soldier in him speaking.

Then Sundance's rifle cracked, the

thunder echoing and drumming across the canyon and through the pass. The bullet tore the rifle out of Gabe's grip and he shook a numbed hand, yelling curses as much from shock as hurt.

The other three scattered, two men blazing wildly into the pass. The bullets ricocheted from the walls harmlessly and Sundance smiled tightly as he pumped two more shots into the canyon to hurry them along.

"Goddamnit, Sundance!" yelled Spooner. "Hold up there! We only want you to ride back with us!"

"Take me alive you mean? What for, Gabe? So's the Colonel can turn loose his hardcases and beat me till he finds out what he wants to know? I've seen his work before!"

Gabe was silent for a moment. "Well, he's curious, I gotta admit that. We all are."

"How many of you were with him at Keystone?"

"You got it wrong. The Colonel was never at Keystone."

"No? Then his men were following his orders."

There was no reply to that for a while. "It was war, Sundance. Everyone done somethin' he's ashamed of."

"Sick of hearing that catch-cry, Gabe. It don't bring back the dead, not a single one."

"Is that what this is all about, the dead?"

"No. The living. Me."

"Christ, who *are* you?"

No reply. Because Sundance realized Gabe was keeping him talking for a purpose. And there was a small trickle of stones and dust from somewhere above his rock. He leaned his shoulders against the rock, lifted the rifle, face close to the pass wall. Something moved across the stars. There was a glint of gunmetal lowering towards him. Sundance fired and a man yelled and then screamed.

Sundance pressed back hard as a body hurtled past him, bounced off the rock and tumbled down into the pass. He heard his chestnut whinny and stomp and knew the man must have landed close.

"Goddamnit, Sundance, I said we only want to talk!"

"That's the advantage I have, Gabe. I don't. And next man you try to have drop on me gets the same as that one down in the pass. One of you can come drag him out if you want. No guns — I'll be covering you all the way. Come on!"

There was silence, a murmur of low voices and then the wounded man gasped, "Someone — come — I'm all busted up!"

Mitch swore and then he raised his voice. "OK, Reb — I'm comin' in to get Pony. Hands empty."

"They better be!"

Sundance kept to the shadows of the rock, watching as Mitch came in warily, empty hands held shoulder high. He could see the man had shucked his gunbelt. Then, as Mitch approached the moaning Pony, Sundance watched the canyon again, saw a moving shadow. Either Gabe or the fourth man.

"Stay put!" he yelled and the shadow froze. "Gabe — you move out where I can see you."

"Go to hell! You ain't callin' the shots here."

"Looks like it to me — but you stay where you are if you want. Just be warned, either of you start up here, you're dead men."

Pony screamed as Mitch got his hands under his arms and began to drag him out of the pass, swearing. Pony kept yelling and cussing with the pain of his wound and his broken leg. Sundance watched them reach the canyon and then Mitch — at a call from Gabe — hurriedly ducked behind the rock there, Pony passing out with a scream.

Sundance ducked and just in time. Gabe had been apparently drawing a bead on his rock, allowing his eyes to become used to the darkness, and his shot was mighty close, whining off Sundance's shelter and showering him with dust. He started up to reply and the second bullet flicked the brim of his hat. He ducked, came up swiftly and hammered three fast shots at the gun flash.

Gabe yelled, startled, and the lead whined away like wild bees in a brushfire. Sundance glimpsed him then, fired once more and Gabe, clambering down from where he had climbed up on a rock, slipped and fell. The fourth man ran forward, crouching, rifle butt braced into his hip, firing and levering as he moved.

Sundance peppered the ground around his boots and the man stopped, started back and, confused, changed his mind and moved sideways. Sundance's next shot took off a bootheel and the man's leg kicked out from under him and he went down. He rolled frantically as more lead spurted dust around him.

Sundance swung the smoking rifle barrel to the canyon entrance in time to see Mitch catch his rifle thrown to him by Gabe who had crawled to more or less safety now. Mitch levered, on one knee, angled the weapon up towards the pass wall.

Sundance had dropped over the edge after his fusillade and as Mitch fired at his old hiding place, he triggered and Mitch spun away, grabbing at a shoulder.

Sundance stood with boots planted wide, covering the J-Link-H men.

"Go back and tell the Colonel I'll talk with him when I'm ready . . . about Keystone and that silver tray and maybe one or two other things."

"By hell, if Hammer hadn't specially told me to bring you in alive, I'd finish you!" growled Gabe Spooner, favouring one leg after his sprawling fall.

"Tell him what I said, Gabe. Now that's all I'm saying right now . . . get Pony across a hoss, without its saddle, and leave the others. You can walk in."

"Christ, man, it's seven miles!"

protested Mitch.

"You want to carry Pony, too, just keep arguing."

They knew when they were licked and swore mostly under their breaths when he made them drop their weapons in a heap. Then he mounted the chestnut and walked it after them a'ways as they started out across the canyon.

He waited until they disappeared into the darkness and then he turned back into the pass, reloading the Winchester's magazine as he walked the horse slowly, finally sheathing the rifle.

Then he drove the three mounts ahead of him after throwing off their saddles and when they came out of the pass into the eastern canyon, he fired a shot into the air, scattering them.

He rode on across the canyon and out the far entrance, pausing just outside, and looked down into the bottom lands. He could make out the dark bulk of some of the homesteaders' cabins, but no lights were showing at this late hour.

Then, just as he was about to heel his horse forward, a gun hammer clicked off to his right and he tripped in the saddle, already halfway out on the far side to the sound, palming up the Smith and Wesson.

"Don't! I've got you covered and I can't miss at this range!"

It was a woman's voice.

That as much as anything stopped his movement and he heaved back upright, letting the pistol slip back into his holster. He made a token move of lifting his hands just above waist level.

"Out kinda late, ain't you, lady?"

"With that accent you must be the Johnny Reb who's caused something of a stir since arriving here — Sundance, isn't it?"

"That's me — and you're . . . ?"

She hesitated, then said, "Kit Dunson. I have a place along Storm Creek and I came to investigate all the shooting.

90

The canyon at this end acts like a megaphone for whatever's happening in the pass. I heard a good deal of gunfire."

"I traded a little lead with Gabe Spooner and some of his men."

"Oh? I thought you were the white-haired boy out at J-Link-H after rescuing Rachel."

He thought he detected a mite of scorn when she spoke the girl's name. "You're well informed, Miss Dunson."

"Mrs," she corrected him, adding belatedly, "Widow Dunson I guess would be more correct."

She had nothing to say about being well informed or otherwise and he filed that away, remembering, hearing a few words that had meant nothing at the time when they were spoken by some of Hammer's men over a desultory card game while awaiting their supper — but now recalling that 'Dunson' was mentioned and someone had said "Morg's widder-woman!" and there had been a gale of dirty laughter.

But he said nothing about that now, his eyes having grown used enough to the night to see her sitting a grey horse with light-coloured stone walls at her back.

"They threw me off, Mrs Dunson, because I slugged Morg after he tried to draw his gun on me."

He heard her breath hiss in. "I — Someone said he'd killed a man in town . . ."

"Seems so. Over a whore — or, leastways, in a whore's room, was what I was given to understand."

"*Damn him!*" The words were hissed and he doubted that she realized she had spoken them aloud, but it helped confirm a suspicion that was forming in Sundance's head.

"You're riding out then?" she said after a silence.

"Out of J-Link-H, anyway — reckon I might stick around a spell before quitting this country altogether."

"For a man who supposedly hates cold weather, Sundance, you don't seem in that much of a hurry to get back to Texas or wherever you come from."

"Have a little business that needs tending to first."

She waited but he did not explain further. "Well, I suppose I'm out of step with everyone else but then I usually am — you can stay at my place tonight if you've a mind: there's room in the bunkhouse . . . lots of room, thanks to Colonel Hammer."

"I'm obliged, Mrs Dunson — but I don't get what you mean about the Colonel."

"Oh, it's simple enough — his men keep beating up my men and they soon get enough and ride on. I'm down to two hands right now and I can run six comfortably."

"Maybe I can make three — I grew up on a farm."

He saw her pause as she started to lower the rifle. She didn't raise it again, but also didn't lower it any further. "Well, I'll have to think about that — but we can talk tomorrow. It's late and I know I'm missing my sleep."

She turned her grey and started to ride down a trail that led into the bottomlands along Storm Creek.

Sundance heeled the chestnut forward and followed silently.

6

Reluctant Avenger

THE Colonel's eyes were bulging as he stood behind his desk, fists resting on the edge, arms trembling a little with the tension, as he glared at Gabe.

"It's gotta be him, Colonel. He knew about the tray. Where it come from and so on . . . he told me he'd quit the trail herd 'cause he'd had a row with the trail boss — ain't so. One of the boys found out he quit because he recognized that bullet gouge under the tray — I tell you, Colonel, it has to be him."

"But he was only a kid and he not only got shot, he burned in the fire!" Hammer's voice lifted in his agitation. He struck the desk with one of his fists.

Gabe sank into a chair. He was mighty weary. After Sundance had set them afoot, he had Pony lifted off the horse and he had ridden in here bareback, sent men with horses for the others and first aid gear for tending to Pony. He also said if he was too bad to get him into town to a doctor.

He had been going to turn in right away but saw the light in the Colonel's den and knew the man would be waiting for a report.

"Colonel, that's what was *s'posed* to've happened. We dunno for sure — and he's about the right age. It was ten years ago, you know."

The Colonel sat down slowly, frowning as he nodded. "Of all the goddamn luck! I knew that tray should never've been put in the store window, but . . . "

He let it trail off but Gabe knew why he had agreed to it. It boosted his ego, kept reminding folk hereabouts that he was a hero, had been loved by his men, had been mentioned in despatches by Sherman himself.

Well, some of it was true, of course, but not all. Not . . .

"If he rides out for Texas there's no more problem," Hammer said suddenly.

Gabe shook his head. "Can't depend on him goin'. I figure he'll stick around if he's who we think he is. He's here for revenge, Colonel. Only way to stop him is with a bullet."

Hammer snapped his head up. "No. It might come to that, but not yet. If I could just talk with him . . . "

Gabe saw the accusation of failure on the man's face and shrugged. "He was too good for us, is all. Caught us nappin' — he won't next time."

"Well, you get a man checking him out, where he's gone, what he's doing. Then we'll decide."

Gabe heaved to his feet, yawning. He had removed his boots to ease his aching feet and crossed to the door, opening it as he said, "Well, I'm turnin' in . . . "

He stopped abruptly, jaw sagging as

he stared at Rachel, standing side on to the door as if she had had her ear pressed against the woodwork. It brought the Colonel to his feet.

"What in blazes're you doing there, girl? You're not s'posed to be out of bed!"

Rachel looked pale, her bruises and abrasions showing more clearly now against her skin. She drew herself up, recovering from her own shock, swayed a little. Gabe moved to steady her and she gave him a quick smile.

"I — didn't mean to eavesdrop. Morg told me what Sundance did to him and that Gabe had kicked him off and that you'd sent Gabe after him — I couldn't sleep and saw Gabe ride in and came down to see what had happened."

They got her into a chair and the Colonel poured her a glass of sherry, jerked his head at Spooner. The foreman went reluctantly, closing the door behind him gently.

"You could've fallen down the stairs!"

Hammer said irritably.

"I held tightly to the rail, father . . . " She drained the sherry, held the glass, turning the stem slowly between her small hands. "I wish Gabe hadn't fired Sundance."

"He gunwhipped your brother!"

"If I know Morg he deserved it . . . but I wanted to thank Sundance properly for what he did."

"He's been thanked — we let him ride out of here in one piece."

The girl held her father's angry gaze. "But you wish he hadn't, don't you? You're afraid of him, father."

Hammer flushed. "Be quiet, girl! Don't you speak to me like that. Now you get on back to bed — I'll help you. The sherry'll put you to sleep."

"No, not yet — I think you owe me some sort of explanation. About Sundance. It's obvious you and Gabe know who he really is and you're both worried — if not actually scared. I'd like to know why."

He took her by the shoulders,

ignoring her wince of pain, and pulled her to her feet, turning her towards the door. "*Peaches!*" he bellowed, calling the Indian woman servant, and when she came hurrying, pulling a colourful blanket about her wide shoulders, her flat face registering surprise at sight of Rachel, Hammer snapped, "Take her back to bed and sleep outside the door. She's not to leave her room again until I say so. Understand?"

"Father . . . !"

"Do like I say, girl!"

He watched, nostrils flaring, breath hissing, as Peaches led her mistress slowly away towards the stairs. He slammed the door and punched one of the heavy panels, ignoring the pain.

It had already started! This damn Sundance had already driven the thin end of the wedge between himself and his family, even if the son of a bitch didn't know it.

Well, it couldn't be allowed to get any worse. The man mightn't realize it, but he could ruin him, turning up just at this time.

Goddamn the luck!

★ ★ ★

The two men employed by Kit Dunson were Bill Merry and Monte Iliffe. They were locals and regarded Sundance with some suspicion, but were not openly hostile to him just because he was a Reb: more because Kit seemed to favour him.

It seemed that Kit and her men ate in the covered dog-run between the house kitchen and the bunkhouse and Sundance was surprised to see she was in her late thirties. Green eyed, hair fair as his own and a good figure for a woman of that age living the hard life she did, but she was not exactly beautiful.

He wouldn't call her homely, more 'plain'. She had some worry lines around her mouth and seemed kind of edgy to him as he commented

101

favourably on her hotcakes and syrup with a knob of home-churned butter melting on top.

"You spoil your men, Mrs Dunson, with food like this."

She smiled faintly, pleased. "They work hard. A man should be fed well — about what you said last night, Sundance, about making up my third hand. I'm still not sure, but I'll take you on temporarily for a few days. We have some stubborn tree stumps to move and we can use the extra muscle, right Monte?"

Monte Iliffe was a man in his forties, hard eyed, hard muscled, lean as a rake handle. He glanced first at Sundance, then nodded to his boss. "Whatever you say, Kit."

"Of course — Bill, will you ride across to Garth Tyson's right after breakfast and tell him I need that chain harness back?"

"Sure, Kit." Merry looked soft and had a bit of a belly on him, but he studied Sundance with narrowed eyes that showed a trace of meanness. "Reckon Monte and me can handle them stumps, though."

"You've been trying to 'handle' them for three days, Bill. An extra pair of hands may make all the difference." She stood and it seemed to be the signal for the others to finish up.

Monte and Bill gulped coffee, moved off, cramming the last of their flapjacks into their mouths. Sundance cut into his last one, looked up at the girl. She watched him, then sat down again.

"You said you had some business to do before you leave . . . yet you offered to work for me. Does the business have anything to do with the Colonel?"

He ate slowly, washed the food down with some coffee. He had made a decision in the last few moments, one he hadn't considered: it had just jumped into his head, fully formed.

"My real name's Cole Travis. Sundance is a name I picked up in Texas after I spent some time with the Comanche. I come from Alma,

Georgia, on a plantation just outside of town, place called Keystone."

Kit Dunson leaned across the plank table and lifted the string and tab of his tobacco sack from his shirt pocket. He was mildly surprised to see her roll a smoke and automatically took out a vesta and snapped it into flame on his thumbnail for her.

"Alma? I've seen that name somewhere . . . "

"Engraved on Colonel Hammer's tray in Holloway's in Cheyenne."

"Yes, of course, the silver coffee set presented to him by his men . . . why're you shaking your head like that? I was there, saw the presentation — in Cheyenne."

"The set was stolen from Keystone during Sherman's march through Georgia. He turned his officers loose to burn and loot the entire State, to teach the Rebs a lesson."

Kit frowned. "I know my recent history. My husband fought for the north, and I had brothers in uniform."

104

Draining his coffee cup, Sundance picked up his tobacco sack, rolled himself a smoke and got it going. He leaned his shoulders back against the wall.

"I fought for the south, naturally. I was pretty young, barely seventeen, when I joined up. I saw a bit of action, then I was detailed to escort a bunch of prisoners to Andersonville. They kept me there as a guard for a while . . . " *His voice drifted off a little as he remembered old Fiddler and all the veteran had taught him during their short time together . . .*

Then had come the day when they culled the prison guards and sent them back into action because the south was so short of men. Fiddler and young Cole Travis were amongst those who went up against the might of Sherman's military machine.

The battalion ran into an ambush in Vidalia Wood, Yankee cannon blasting out of the trees where they were hidden at close range, blowing men and horses to shreds in spurts of flame and smoke. Musket fire rattled continuously, cutting down the infantry like a scythe through wheat. The Rebs were routed, ran in panic, most throwing away their weapons, including Travis. But Fiddler picked up his rifle and rammed it back into his hands.

"Don't be a fool, boy! We ain't outta this yet!"

Fiddler led the way and a dozen or more followed blindly. He knew the country, got them away from the main Yankee assault — but ran them into reinforcements on the way to the battle front. Muskets rattled again, interspersed with the deep boom of Spencer repeaters. The Rebs were cut down and the Yankees, fired up by victory, gave chase with fixed bayonets.

Fiddler helped young Travis fix his own bayonet to the rifle muzzle, the younger man's hands shaking too badly to manage it. They were cornered and they turned like rats in a trap and faced the charging Yanks.

They fired their rifles, dropped two men. Three other survivors brought down bluecoats, too, and then the wall of stabbing steel was on them. Travis's meagre training came to his rescue and he parried and thrust, missed with the blade but brought the butt of his heavy issue musket around and smashed the Yankee's jaw for him. Fiddler ran a man through and placed his boot against the blue uniform coat to pull the bayonet free.

Travis spun left and his eyes widened as he saw a Yankee with his rifle to his shoulder not six feet away, aiming for his chest dead centre. As the muzzle spurted smoke and flame, Fiddler's body appeared before him, shuddered as the ball meant for him smashed into the old guard. Blind fury took hold of Travis and he leapt over Fiddler's falling body, ran the Yankee through, withdrew and stabbed again, and again.

Then he felt the searing pain of a

bayonet piercing his side and he fell into blackness, his blood spilling . . .

When he came to, he was covered by piles of dead men and the sound of fighting was far away. He had lost a deal of blood and crawled to where Fiddler lay in the rain, eyes half open, mouth agape revealing his rotten teeth, half full of congealed dark blood. Travis threw up, and he didn't know how much longer it was before he crawled about, took a first aid kit from a dead Yankee and poured antiseptic into his bayonet wound and bandaged it roughly.

"*I crawled out of there. I knew where I was* when I saw the Vidalia church spire, even though it was on fire, like the rest of the town," he told the silent Dunson woman slowly. "Alma wasn't that far away, and Keystone was only just beyond . . ."

"You went home? You — deserted?"

He nodded. "I'd been left for dead. There were no Confederates anywhere to be seen. Home seemed like a pretty good idea to me. My mother and sister were there, and we had a houseful of servants who could take care of me."

"Slaves," she said flatly.

He nodded. "That was our way of life, but our slaves were treated well, better than if they'd been free and trying to make their own living. Anyway, that issue's done with. I made it home and Cassie, my sister, found me in the vegetable patch. As it happened there were only two slaves left on Keystone, Dooley and his wife Prissy . . . "

They got him into the house and Cassie and his mother fussed over him, wept over him, prayed over him, thanking the Good Lord for returning him home to them, even in his wounded state.

There were messages coming constantly from neighbours about the Yankees storming across Georgia, putting everything to the torch. Some Yankees had been allowed to go hog-wild, raping and pillaging and murdering women and children, black and white.

But they had a week before Dooley brought word that the Yankees were coming down the road and would be there within minutes.

They could hear their drunken laughter and shouting. They hid the wounded Travis in the cellar, his fully loaded Griswald and Gunnison six-shooter in his hand, propped up behind a screen of barrels on old clothes and pillows.

He pleaded with his mother and Cassie to run and hide but his mother was a proud woman.

"Your father built this place for me, Cole. I will not run and leave it to be desecrated by drunken Yankees — Dooley and Prissy will take Cassie and hide in the swamps, but I intend to stay and do what I can to — Oh, dear God! They're breaking in upstairs! We've left it too late . . . "

It was true. A small bunch of soldiers had already arrived, smashed in the big glass doors, were already ransacking the treasures of the big plantation house.

Mrs Travis, clasping her long-dead husband's brace of pistols, hurried out of the cellar, young Cole Travis calling after her to please *run* for it . . .

The soldiers heard him and soon found him and he shot the first one through the belly, the second in the head. Then the big, bearded sergeant raised a big Dragoon pistol and put a .44 slug into his chest. He fell back and vaguely felt his pistol taken. "You're in for a foretaste of hell, boy!"

"Sarge — we got us two fine-lookin' women upstairs," a coarse, drink-slurred voice called from the floor above. "You wantin' a piece of southern sweetmeat, sarge . . . ?"

"You damn well better save some for me before we burn the place down!" the sergeant growled.

"Aw, we gonna burn a place nice as this, sarge? It's kinda like outta a story book."

"Colonel said rape who you like, steal what you want, even kill if you have to or are of a mind to — but *burn the goddamn evidence and the corpses!* You got it now, O'Reilly?"

"I do, sarge, I got it now . . . but you better hurry man."

"I'll set this cellar a'burnin' before I come up — I'll have time to visit the ladies before we burn the main house."

Travis passed out as he heard the scrape of the first match across the bearded sergeant's trouser's seat . . .

"*Dooley was badly wounded* but he crawled back in through the fire and somehow got me out," Sundance said heavily, his eyes telling Kit his thoughts were a long, long way from her dog-run. "Dooley got me to other survivors and they helped me but he was dying. I got to talk to him before he cashed in . . . "

They were deep in the swamps and the Yankees were afraid to come in here because of snakes and the occasional 'gator. They were about as safe as they could ever be at that time.

Dooley's face was grey and the crude

bandages covering the awful raw wound in the side of his chest were soaked with blood.

Travis's own chest was bandaged but he had been lucky — the lead ball had skidded off a rib, ripping up a lot of flesh and bleeding plenty, but far from fatal.

"Mister Cole — they done stole lots of things," the dying negro rasped, ignoring Travis's admonition to hush and rest. "So many things — Mrs T's jewl'ry. My Prissy's brooch your mammy done give her on her birthday, so much . . ."

"It's all right, Dooley. It's all right."

The old negro began to cry because he hadn't been able to save Prissy or Cassie or Travis's mother. They had been raped and shot and left to burn in the blazing house . . .

Young Travis's jaw knotted with muscle as he clenched his teeth, tried to put from his mind the terrible images that had begun to form there.

"Mister Cole — they even tooken

your Daddy's silver coffee set that belonged to *his* Daddy an' Mammy. I heard that sergeant say it'd make a nice gift for Colonel Harmer . . . They oughtn't tooken it like that, Mister Cole, not somethin'd been in your family so — many — years . . . "

Sundance stopped, stared at the burning stub of his cigarette, flicked it away out of the dog-run area.

"I wasted a lot of time trying to track down a Colonel 'Harmer'," he said finally. "I hadn't allowed for Dooley's accent, you see?"

Kit Dunson, a little pale and her eyes compassionate, reached across the table and squeezed his hand gently. "Then the other day you saw that same coffee set in Holloway's window with the engraving . . . "

He nodded. "Soon as I saw 'Colonel Hammer' I knew he was the one I'd been looking for. 'Hammer' not 'Harmer'. I *knew* it."

"But he wasn't actually at Keystone was he?"

"No. But his men were acting on his orders. In fact, he'd just given them an open invitation go to rape and murder and steal. In my book, he's more guilty than his men."

She frowned, drawing her hand away slowly. "You're after revenge?"

He looked at her with his smoky eyes. "Damn right."

"Well, I have little time for Jacob Hammer. He's greedy and arrogant and determined to drive us homesteaders out. D'you think you'll feel satisfied with revenge?"

"I'll feel satisfied when I've squared things — I'm bound to do it, Mrs Dunson. Southern honour, if you want to call it that. But my mother and sister died terrible deaths. So did Prissy. Dooley gave his life to save me . . . I can't go to my grave without making some try at avenging them."

"You've been trying for ten years?"

He shook his head. "No. I gave up after three years. I tracked down some Colonel 'Harmer's but none of them fitted the bill. I didn't have any other names, not even the sergeant's. And there could've been several 'sergeants' under a Colonel's command . . . I decided to get on with my own life but if the chance arose where I might just find my man, I'd grab it."

"And it happened in Cheyenne?"

He nodded. "Now you know why I'm sticking around. If you don't care for it — and I won't blame you — then I'll move out — but I'll still be around the basin."

"Oh, I wouldn't want you to move out," Kit Dunson said. "It'll be to my advantage to have an enemy of Colonel Hammer's working for me — I have reason to hate the man's guts and he's also trying to drive me out, me and the other homesteaders . . . Hellfire Pass is the only way in and out of Medicine Basin, you see. He wants our land so he can fatten his cattle here on this side of the range before driving them to market — and I'll be damned if he's going to get my place."

"Yeah, well he kind of hinted he might have me front for him and buy homesteaders' land, then I could work it for him."

"And you refused?"

"Didn't say one way or another. If it would've served my purpose, I'd've taken up his offer."

She stood slowly, smiling crookedly. "I think we understand each other, Sundance . . . You have a job here for as long it takes you to do — whatever it is you aim to do to Colonel Hammer." She thrust out her right hand suddenly. "Deal?"

He stood slowly, studied her briefly, then nodded and gripped hands with her. "We have a deal. But I do things my way, in my time."

Her mouth tightened a little and then she said, "By the way, you've probably guessed that Gabe Spooner was the Colonel's sergeant during the war. He used to wear a beard, too."

Sundance had suspected that Spooner could be the man he was after, but he didn't care for the way the woman seemed to think she could use him for her own ends.

Whatever else he was, he was no one's hired killer.

7

Time to Die

MORGAN HAMMER was surly at breakfast and growled at Peaches, complaining about the food.

"And where's my father? Why ain't he here at table?"

"Colonel in office," the Indian woman told him, her face carefully blank, showing no outward sign of the anger she felt at his rasping insults about her race.

Morgan stood abruptly with a curse, knocking his chair over and leaving it on the floor as he downed the rest of his coffee and strode angrily from the room. He found his father seated at his desk, studying a leather-bound book with pages tattered on their edges. The Colonel looked up irritably.

"How many times do I have to tell you to knock before entering this room! *Any* room!"

"Sorry," Morgan said automatically and stood edgily in front of the desk, one hand tapping against his gun butt. "I want to know what we're doin' about this Reb, Sundance . . . I hear that he gave old Gabe the slip last night."

"Gabe was over-confident. It won't happen again."

"Over-age, you mean. Time you pensioned him off, Pa, and let me run the spread."

The Colonel sat back in his chair, lips pursed. "Not yet, boy — you've plenty to learn and if you pay attention to Gabe Spooner you'll be the better for it. Best sergeant I ever had."

"But you kept him a sergeant! Why didn't you promote him to lieutenant or something if he was so blamed good?"

"Some men excel in certain positions. Oh, they may be good in higher ones, but they seem to reach their peak at a certain level and it's best to leave them there — you'd understand that if you tried better to understand *people*, boy, instead of going off half-cocked all the time and relying on me to pull you out of the trouble you get yourself into."

Morgan scowled but hid it by turning away and dropping into a chair. He had removed the bandage from his head today and the swelling and small cut from Sundance's gun barrel were obvious. He was a good-looking young man in a surly way, but baby-faced enough to make women want to tote him in their arms. And Morg took full advantage of that fact.

"Pa, let's get back to Sundance . . . I looked in on Rachel this morning and she told me he's got you and old Gabe buffaloed . . . "

"That damn girl! She eavesdropped last night — and no one has me 'buffaloed'."

"Well, she seems convinced you're scared of Sundance for some reason.

If he's gonna be trouble, whyn't you let me take care of him?" He slapped his gun butt. "I'm good with this and I got reason to call him out — you could keep the marshal off my neck if you made enough of a fuss."

He had expected an explosion but the Colonel frowned and steepled his long fingers, looking through them at his son. "At times you show some possibilities, Morgan. But it's not time for gunplay. And I'm not sure about the marshal but he can be taken care of in lots of ways when need be — No, for now we wait. Skeets has taken Pony into town to a doctor's. He's going to find out where Sundance went and what he's up to. After he gets back, you come see me again and we might work something out."

Morgan grinned, his heart pounding with excitement. This was the last thing he had expected from his father.

It meant that Sundance really did have the old man scared white, no matter what he said. He'd sure like to know why, but now wasn't the time to push it.

He dropped his gaze to the old book in front of the Colonel. Looked like it could be a journal. It was kept in the safe in a locked leather valise.

But he had found out a long time back where the safe key was kept and that he could open the valise with one of Rachel's hair pins. At the time he had been only interested in money and hadn't bothered looking in the book.

But maybe later when his father was out on the range . . .

★ ★ ★

Sundance straightened and leaned on his shovel handle, mopping sweat from his face and dirt-caked torso with a balled rag. Amongst the ridged muscles on his chest and ribs, there were two scars, a long, ragged one on the left side and lower down the puckered one left by the Yankee bayonet. He glanced across the stubborn stump at Bill

Merry. Monte Iliffe was busy hitching a chain around a second stump some yards away.

"This is gonna take dynamite."

Merry snapped his gaze at him and stopped using the pickaxe, panting, his soft belly jiggling with his movements. "Mister, you forget about explosives. You're only here temporarily. Me an' Monte, this is our living . . . longer we take to do a job, longer we're employed. Kit ain't got a heap of money and we got us an idea that soon as we get her land cleared and ploughed, Monte and me're gonna have to start lookin' for a winter berth — and, I tell you true, that ain't a lot of fun up here. All the winter jobs're taken mighty early. So, you just let us fuss along in our own way. We'll have these stumps out in our own time, when it's a mite late for Kit to decently fire us."

Monte heard Merry's words and strolled across, wiping his calloused hands on a dirty rag. His hard eyes found Sundance's but he saw little friendliness there.

"You poke your nose in where it ain't wanted, Reb, and they'll ship you back to Texas in a pine box."

Both men were ganged up on him now, facing him, Merry holding the pick half raised across his chest, Iliffe with his boots set for a fight.

Sundance smiled faintly. "Seems I stomped all over your nice little set-up, eh? Noticed the porch rails and steps and doors and window frames were all painted up real purty. Little picket fence around the flower garden at the side, stone-laid path out to the privy from the back door . . . you boys've been kept real busy, right?"

"We're makin' the place real nice for Kit," Merry said with a touch of indignation at any suggestion he and Iliffe had been marking time. "It's the way she likes it. Her husband would never waste time on it and so now . . . "

"You're breaking my heart, Merry,"

cut in Sundance. "Couple of old daisies, the pair of you . . . letting go the real work, keeping Kit satisfied by prettying the place up — and being paid for it, too."

Monte Iliffe suddenly stepped forward, swinging a looping right. "No one calls me a daisy!"

Sundance blocked the blow, his own right exploding against Monte's jaw. The man stumbled back half a dozen paces, sat down, slid part way into the stump hole. Bill Merry swore and swung the pick. Or started to. Sundance went in under the tool and hit him two blurring blows on that soft gut. The breath whooshed out of the man and he sat down, the pick in his lap as he retched and fought for breath.

Monte Iliffe was struggling out of the stump hole, rock in his fist. Sundance kicked him almost lazily in the chest and the man rolled back into the hole, gagging.

Sundance shook his head, slowly.

"No wonder the Colonel's men never bothered to beat up on you two — they knew damn well you weren't doing Kit any good. I'm just surprised she never saw it . . . "

But she knew. When he rode back to the house and told her the stumps could be dynamited and cleared by sundown, he saw by her face that she knew full well the other two had been letting go the real work just to pretty up the place.

She sighed. "I knew that if I fired them and hired someone else to replace them — that's if anyone from around here would be foolish enough to hire on — they'd be beaten up by Hammer's men. Once in a while I manage to get Bill and Monte out into the fields or fixing fences or doing other work that becomes essential. I — compromised and it rather galls me to know that Hammer *allowed* Bill and Monte to work for me. One word from him and they'd be laid up in Doc Gibson's infirmary."

"Well, how you run your place is up to you — but if you want those stumps out and that land cleared by winter, it's going to take dynamite."

She studied him carefully. "You know how to handle explosives?"

"I did some during the war. I'm no expert but I can blow a stump without losing my hands."

After a short deliberation she nodded. "All right — I'll give you a note to Holloway. His is the only store that sells dynamite."

A half hour later, Bill Merry and Monte Iliffe, resting and smoking on one of the big cedar stumps, watched as Sundance rode out of the yard on his chestnut, leading a dun packhorse.

"Sonovabitch's gonna get that dynamite!" Monte hissed. "You an' me'll be lucky if we still have a job come winter, Bill."

"Don't worry," Merry said, rubbing his sore midriff. "We'll be all right. But I wouldn't bet on that Reb bein' around to see it."

Iliffe snapped his head around, looking startled. He had never heard flabby Bill Merry speak with such venom.

★ ★ ★

The man called Skeets skidded his mount in the yard of the J-Link-H, watched by Rachel through the lace curtains of her bedroom window. Sitting somewhat stiffly and uncomfortably in a straightback chair, the girl frowned: Skeets was not a ranch hand who generally was in a hurry to do anything, but he sure seemed to have a bug in his ear right now.

He quit the saddle before the animal had stopped moving, tossed the reins carelessly in the general direction of the corral poles and ignored the shouted queries of men working on the barn. He sprinted for the house and then Rachel lost sight of him.

She would have liked to have crept downstairs and listened outside her father's office door again but she was locked in her room now and there was nothing she could do about it.

If she could have stamped her small foot without it jarring through her bruised body and hurting so much, she would have.

She would dearly like to know just who this Sundance was and why her father and Gabe Spooner were so scared of him . . .

Maybe if Morg came to visit her again, she might be able to slyly nudge his curiosity and get him to find out for her . . .

But Morgan and Gabe Spooner were in the Colonel's office when Skeets came hurrying in, reeking of sweat and horses. Hammer twitched his nostrils.

"Boss — that Sundance feller wasn't in town when I took Pony to the doc's — he'll be laid up a spell with a busted leg and a bullet wound in his backside — I asked in the saloon and no one had seen Sundance, but when I was comin' out, I spotted him pullin' away from Holloway's, leading a pack hoss with something under burlap. I asked Holloway what he'd bought and you'll just love this . . . " He paused for effect but found no encouragement in the eyes of the waiting men. He swallowed. "He bought half a case of dynamite, couple coils of fuse and two boxes of detonators."

"Judas priest!" breathed Gabe Spooner, looking sharply at the Colonel.

Morgan frowned, seeming a little puzzled.

"Says he wants to blow some stumps for Kit Dunson," Skeets added, disappointed he hadn't been able to make his announcement any more dramatic. But the effects weren't bad . . .

Hammer nodded. "Help yourself to a drink, Skeets, then go get cleaned up. You're offensive."

Skeets coloured but poured a very big whiskey and downed it in a couple of gulps. He nodded, unable to speak, his eyes watering, as he hurried out.

Colonel Hammer ordered Morgan to

open the window wider, then sat down behind his desk.

He raised his eyes to Spooner. "Half a case — a man could blow a lot of tree stumps with that much dynamite, Gabe."

"Lot of tree stumps — or the walls of Hellfire Pass," Spooner said grimly and suddenly Morgan didn't look puzzled any more, understanding now why his father and Gabe had looked so alarmed at Skeets' news.

"Hell, you really figure he's about to seal off the pass, pa?"

"D'you really figure we can take the chance he's not going to blast it down, boy?"

Morgan frowned. He was about to say he could find out for sure from Kit Dunson but stopped himself in time. Hell, if his father found out he was seeing her . . .

"Kit and them other homesteaders must've hired him to fight for 'em," Spooner suggested.

Hammer nodded slow agreement.

"It's possible. But we can't spend time trying to work out the whys and wherefores now. We've got to make sure that damn Johnny Reb doesn't seal us in here for the winter — and a lot longer!" He flicked his eyes to Gabe. "Mitch's shoulder's not too bad is it? He was something of a sharp-shooter during the war. None too bright, but a good shot and a good hater — fetch him in, Gabe."

As Spooner went out, Morgan confronted his father.

"Damn, pa, I thought you said if Sundance needed killin', the job was mine?"

Hammer shook his head. "I said you had a good enough notion, making it look like a personal thing between you — that's OK for in town where there're plenty of witnesses who'll back you up, but out on the range, it can too easily be turned around to look like straight murder — and you know that Marshal Ty Monroe can — and will — do it."

"Sundance is pretty fast. S'pose he gets Mitch first?"

Colonel Hammer frowned and tapped his fingers against his silver belt buckle. "Mmmm — possible, I s'pose, but Mitch usually makes a long shot. I've seen him hit a man smack between the eyes from four hundred yards and . . . "

"Pa!"

Hammer stopped speaking, arched his eyebrows at Morg's tone. He nodded gently. "All right — you know I get carried away sometimes when I start to reminisce about the war."

"I'm as good a shot as Mitch with that new '73 Winchester you bought me for my last birthday . . . Pa, I *want* Sundance! — I owe the son of a bitch, you know I do!"

The Colonel sighed. "All right, all right, you go with Mitch — but only as back-up, mind. I'd rather you weren't involved too deeply — Ah, here's Mitch now . . . just how badly d'you hate Sundance's guts, Mitch, old friend . . . ?"

★ ★ ★

Bill Merry and Monte Iliffe were still surly after the brief fight and weren't about to help Sundance blow the stumps. "Kit'll find you some painting or gardening to do," Sundance told them disdainfully. "I don't need you two."

"Hope you blow your lousy head off!" growled Merry and Iliffe seconded that.

Sundance grinned, took a stick of dynamite and tossed it up into the air, deliberately fumbling the catch. The two hands almost ran from Kit's barn. She appeared shortly after, face tight.

"Seems you aren't hitting it off with those two."

"I dunno where you found 'em but they don't seem to want to work hard. Don't know much, either. Ran like hell when I pretended to drop a stick of dynamite . . . didn't even have a detonator in it."

She was looking at the explosives he had laid out on an old burlap bag on the dirt floor. Fuses protruded from half a dozen sticks. "Are they ready to use?"

He nodded. "Two sticks for each stump ought to do it easy but I'll make extras. You'll have a deal left over."

Kit avoided his eyes. "I — daresay I'll find a use for it. I want to make some irrigation channels from the creek for my crops, get ready for the spring thaw. It'll be quicker and easier to blast than try to dig frozen ground."

"Uh-huh." That was Sundance's only comment and he stowed the unused explosive back in the wooden box with the fuses, keeping the detonators separate. She showed him a dusty back shelf where he placed the box and the detonators and covered it with some more old gunnysacks.

He gathered up his dynamite in the

burlap bag and Kit tensed visibly.

"It's safe enough now. I'll blow the stumps and be back in time for supper, maybe just a little late . . . "

"Be careful."

He grunted and they left the barn together, the girl seeming glad to be able to go back to the house while he mounted the chestnut and rode through the afternoon haze to the flatland where the stubborn stumps were, the foothills rising behind. He dismounted and placed his first charges and the stump was blown free of the heavy root system in a few minutes. It sagged to one side and was obviously ready to be dug and rolled out of the hole.

He moved along to the next stump, bigger and more difficult . . .

Up in the rocks of the foothills of the Storm Creek Range, Mitch settled himself more comfortably and opened the breech of his Sharps Big Fifty buffalo rifle, thumbing in the big two-and-three-quarter-inch cartridge with its blunt-nose lead bullet. It would mushroom when it hit flesh and bone, destroying organs, leaving an exit wound a man could poke his fist through.

Mitch was happy with this chore. His shoulder was giving him hell but at least it wasn't the one that would be jarred by the heavy calibre rifle when he squeezed off his shot.

It didn't matter to him that Sundance wasn't using the dynamite to blow down Hellfire Pass and seal off Medicine Basin. He owed this damn southerner and he aimed to make the most of it. Blow his goddamn head clear off his shoulders . . .

He sighted steadily as Sundance knelt beside the second stump and began digging a hole for the placement of the dynamite.

Yeah . . . head resting beautifully in the buckhorn of the rear sight, balanced neatly atop the blade foresight. His finger took up the slack in the double-set trigger, taking it right back to where it was ready to trip and fire.

Then he saw Bill Merry and Monte Iliffe . . .

"What in the hell!" Mitch swore, lowering the rifle, frowning as he watched the two men below creep through the rocks between his position and Sundance.

He looked around for Morg but the man was holed up somewhere out of sight.

"Judas priest!" Mitch O'Reilly breathed as he saw Sundance, warned by some instinct no doubt, start to turn from where he was planting the charge of dynamite. Merry and Iliffe were upon him in an instant, swinging their gun barrels, falling over each other in their eagerness to get at Sundance.

The big tow-headed man was off-balance and only managed to get his Smith and Wesson half clear of leather when he went down under the assault. They kicked him as he lay there and the wind brought Iliffe's snarled words clearly to Mitch.

"We'll show you who's runnin' things around here, you goddamn Reb."

He hefted his rifle for another blow but Merry grabbed his arm. "Ease up, Monte! Just follow the original plan — go bring his mount."

Iliffe seemed reluctant to obey but moved off and then Mitch heard a footstep behind him and he spun, bringing around his big buffalo gun awkwardly. He froze as he looked down the barrel of Morg's Winchester. The young man grinned tightly. "Could nail you easy, Mitch. God knows why pa thought you were such a hotshot. You ought've nailed Sundance by now."

"Hell, I was all set to go and then them two old fools showed up — I din' know what to do!"

Morg twisted his mouth as he watched Iliffe appear, leading Sundance's chestnut, and he noted the warbag tied behind the cantle. Looked like the old daisies were going to run Sundance off . . .

"What should we do, Morg?" asked Mitch again.

"I'll show you." And Morg threw his rifle to his shoulder, fired four rapid shots, making Mitch jump, and when O'Reilly looked again, Merry and Iliffe were down, Monte still twitching a little, their clothes splashed with blood.

8

Night Hunt

"FOR God's sake, man! We ain't s'posed to make this a massacre!" Mitch was thrown by Morg's sudden decision to shoot down Merry and Iliffe.

"Use your head. It was a perfect set-up. We just move 'em around a little and make it look like they shot it out and killed each other . . . J-Link-H don't even have to be involved."

Mitch O'Reilly's jaw dropped a little. "Aw, yeah! Hey, good idea, Morg . . . "

The young Hammer grunted and levered a fresh shell into his Winchester's breech. "Let's get on down there — I want to be looking into Sundance's eyes when he gets it."

Mitch wasn't keen on that part but

he knew Morg was smarter than him and, anyway, he *was* the Colonel's son. So he stood up with the buffalo rifle and followed Morg down the slope through the rocks . . .

Sundance's head was ringing and for a moment he thought he must have been standing too close to the dynamite blast but then he remembered he had heard a boot crunch on gravel, spun around in time to see two blurred shapes almost upon him, swinging their gun barrels. He put a shaky hand against his head and felt a little blood and a mighty big swelling there.

His vision was blurred and everything looked to be standing side by side in double image, but he made out a horse waiting with bowed head, saddled, close by — his own chestnut? Beyond he saw two sprawled bodies, one moving slowly. Instinctively, not really understanding exactly what he was doing or why, he groped for his Smith and Wesson pistol down at his side.

"Watch out! He's coming round!"

Sundance snapped his head towards the sound and saw two blurred figures coming out of the rocks, both holding rifles. The old instincts took over as he rolled away, shooting.

Morgan was throwing his rifle to his shoulder, reeled as a bullet grazed his ribs. His rifle exploded into the air and he sat down with a cry and a sob. It wasn't a serious wound but it was the first time he had been struck by a bullet and it scared him.

Mitch fired his buffalo gun from hip-level but he didn't have the butt held tightly against his body and the recoil slammed him off balance, the rifle barrel kicking high as he staggered.

Sundance flopped over onto his belly and the pistol barked twice, Mitch knocked clear off his feet by the strike of lead. Morg Hammer, scared and holding his bleeding side, dropped his rifle and got his legs under him, zigzagging back to the shelter of the rocks. Bullets kicked dust around his feet and he dived headlong over the nearest rock, striking his hip hard enough to make him cry out.

The pistol was empty now and Sundance, still dazed, the world spinning about him, launched himself at his wide-eyed mount's trailing reins, grabbed them and hauled himself to his feet. His knees buckled but he got up again and threw himself bodily across the saddle as Morgan opened up with his Peacemaker, shooting wildly, the bullets striking the tree stump and rocks.

Sundance yelled into the horse's ear and struggled to get his leg across its back as it charged away from the slope, needing no urging as bullets whined and buzzed. Sundance managed to get into the saddle, lay low along the mount's back as it charged on towards the foothills. He gave it its head, hands twisted in the mane as he tried desperately to hold on, his brain spinning . . .

Gun empty, Morg stood, screaming curses, threw down the Peacemaker and ran to where he had dropped his rifle in the dust. He stepped on Mitch as he picked it up, ignoring the man's scream of pain. He fired several shots after the retreating Sundance and then the man was out of sight in amongst the boulders and arroyos of the foothills. Morgan Hammer swore aloud, hands shaking as he reloaded the smoking rifle.

"M-Morg — gimme a — hand — pard — I'm — hit — bad . . . "

Morgan Hammer looked down at the grey-faced Mitch O'Reilly, seeing the large patch of blood on the man's shirt. He sure had more than a shoulder-nick this time . . . He paused, aware that his own wound was hurting, pulled out his bloody shirt and was relieved to see the shallow, bleeding groove cut across the flesh over his lower ribs. His breath hissed out in relief and he turned back to Mitch who was coughing blood now.

"You're finished, Mitch, old pard," he announced with no trace of sympathy in his voice. As the wounded man tried to sit up, Morg got a boot toe under his shoulder and heaved him onto his belly. Mitch's scream was drowned in the rifle's bark as Morg shot him in the back of the head.

Then, whistling soundlessly between his teeth, he walked across to where Merry and Iliffe lay, the latter still alive, clasping his chest. Morg smiled crookedly, walked behind Iliffe and shot him coldly in the back of the head. Merry was already dead, but Morg shot him in the back of the head also, stood back, looking at the three dead men and then down at his own bloody fingers. His smile widened.

"Now then, Mr Johnny Reb Sundance, ain't you in a heap of trouble? Three dead men, all finished off with a bullet in the head, me, honourably wounded — and lucky I got out alive and able to tell the story, huh . . . ?" He laughed aloud, briefly. "Aw, mister, you got more trouble than you can shake a stick at and ain't that just too bad!"

147

* * *

Kit Dunson was in her barn when she heard the horse come into her yard. She hurriedly threw a gunnysack over the dynamite and fuses and detonator caps on the burlap square and snatched up her shotgun. She was surprised to see Morgan Hammer forking his zebra dun, hunched over in the saddle, one side of his shirt all bloody.

"Kit — I need help, I been shot," Morg gasped in his best suffering voice.

Kit hurried forward and quickly set down the shotgun as he almost tumbled out of the saddle. She steadied him, their bodies pressed together against the uneasy horse, and for a moment she thought she saw amusement in Morgan's eyes.

"What happened?" she asked, moving away but holding his arm. He draped it around her shoulders and they started towards the house.

"Sundance shot me."

She stopped abruptly and he stumbled,

148

forced her to keep walking towards the house.

"Mitch heard he was blasting stumps and Mitch was mighty riled because Sundance had wounded him. He said he was gonna square things. I told pa and he sent me after him to head him off." He was gasping for breath now, pleased with his acting as she helped him up the porch steps and into the house. She seated him in the kitchen, fetched hot water and clean rags as he struggled out of his shirt. "I got there too late, Kit — but just in time to see your man walk around behind all three of them and shoot 'em through the back of the head, finishing 'em off."

Frowning and pale, Kit Dunson looked up from where she knelt beside the chair, bathing his wound. "Three of them?"

"Yeah — seemed like Bill Merry and Monte Iliffe had had some sort of argument with him — looked like he'd shot 'em down, nailed Mitch, then went around and finished 'em off."

"But he let you live."

His gaze held her's steadily. "I took a few shots at him and yelled like I had a bunch of men waitin' back in the rocks — he winged me but I must've scared him. He took off for the hills."

Kit frowned, her mouth tight as she worked swiftly, cleaned the wound and bound it up with rags after pouring iodine into it. The sting brought tears to Morg's eyes and he howled, panting wildly.

"Don't be such a baby. It's not much of a wound."

"You might think differently if you had it — look, I need to borrow your buckboard to tote them bodies into the marshal, OK?"

Damn, she thought. It was in the barn and she didn't want Morg Hammer going in there right now and maybe poking about and finding the dynamite . . .

"All right. But you stay here and have a cup of coffee. I'll harness the team."

She was startled when he stood abruptly in front of her and slipped his arms about her waist, pulling her in close, mauling her.

"Like you said, Kit, it ain't much of a wound and it's been a few days since we got together — let's go, huh? Them dead men ain't going no place."

"Neither are you!" she snapped as he kept mauling her and when she couldn't break his grip, she balled a fist and hit him on the wound. He gagged and doubled up, staggering, grabbing the back of a chair to steady himself, whitefaced now.

"God, that *hurt*!"

"It was meant to — now get outside, Morg. You can take the buckboard but have someone else return it. I never want to see you again, here or anywhere else."

His jaw sagged. "Wh — ? *You're* tellin' me you . . . the hell you are! No woman gives me the brushoff. I dump *them* when I'm good and ready . . . "

"Well, I'm telling you, Morg, we're finished."

For a moment he couldn't speak, he was so angry and shocked. "Oh, yeah? And who you gonna get to take my place? A plain, ugly bitch like you — hell, you think I was really interested in you? Judas priest, you stupid bitch, I was only seein' if I could get you to sell your goddamn land to the Colonel so's I could get in his good books! What're you laughin' at, damn you?"

"Using *me*, were you, Morg? Well, *I* was using, *you*, you pathetic little spoiled brat! I was pumping you for information about the Colonel's plans. You have no idea just how much you told me when we were romping together, have you? Why, you poor fool, you told me everything I wanted to know — but I can't stomach you any more, Morg. Now get outside while I fix the buckboard."

She had been moving about while she was speaking and now reached up suddenly and took down her dead husband's deer rifle from the antler-rack above the fireplace. She levered a shell expertly, lowered the barrel to point a little south of the startled Morg's belt buckle.

"Better move, Morg, or you'll never be interested in women again, young or old!"

His eyes blazed murderously, but he slowly moved through the house and out into the yard. She took his Peacemaker before she went into the barn and harnessed the team to the buckboard.

Silently, he tied his dun's reins to the tailgate and grunted as he heaved himself up into the driving seat.

"I won't forget this, Kit," he said quietly and lifted the reins, ready to drive out of the yard, now washed with the fires of sundown. "And neither will you! That's a promise — you old hag!"

Kit felt quite sick as she tossed his pistol into the back of the buckboard — unloaded — and she hugged herself as she watched him clear the yard and drive out towards the darkening hills . . .

Where, according to Morg, Sundance had gone. Well, if he'd run out on her, he was of no use to her. He could take his chances with the posse that Marshal Monroe would no doubt set on his trail.

The hell with him, anyway. She had a plan of her own now.

She turned back into the barn and lit a lantern and slung it on a nail on a post where it would cast its light across the burlap square where the dynamite was.

★ ★ ★

It was dark by the time Morgan Hammer had the bodies loaded into the buckboard and started up the trail to town.

He hadn't gone far when he heard horses coming and his blood ran cold for a moment as he reached down under the seat and grabbed his Winchester.

"Morg? That you?"

He relaxed when he heard his father's anxious voice and as the Colonel and Gabe Spooner ranged alongside, he prepared to put on his best pain-filled look.

"Pa! Am I glad to see you!"

"Jesus, Colonel, there's three dead men in the back, includin' Mitch!" Gabe sounded a mite shaken and Morg smiled inwardly, happy that he had disturbed the tough old ramrod.

The Colonel looked quickly and then back to his son. "We were worried when you and Mitch didn't come back by dark — what the hell happened . . . ? Hell, boy, are you hit?"

Morg grimaced as he let a hand press gently against his bullet-shredded, blood-stained shirt. "Caught one across the ribs from that goddamn Reb — ain't so bad, pa. Kit Dunson doctored me when I went in to borrow her buckboard."

"Kit! The hell you doing going to her, boy?"

"Her place was closest . . . "

"Colonel," broke in Gabe, still looking closely at the dead men. "Two of these are Bill Merry and Monte Iliffe."

Hammer turned grimly to his son. "Better tell us what happened, Morg."

So Morg told the same story as he had told Kit and before the Colonel or Gabe could speak, added quickly, "Pa, we can turn this to our advantage . . . Sundance's hurt some, the way Merry and his pard slugged him. He's a triple murderer now. We tell the marshal and he gets up a posse and durin' the chase we see that he's killed and no one can blame J-Link-H at all."

Gabe and the Colonel were silent for a spell. Then Hammer looked at Gabe and said with a touch of pride, "Now that's thinking, Gabe!"

"Somethin's wrong, Colonel," Spooner said quietly. The others looked at him and he said, "Well, I didn't know Sundance all that well but I can read a man pretty good and I'd say he ain't the kind to gun a man down, then go shootin' him in the back of the head."

"You calling me a liar?" blazed Morgan, dropping a hand to his gun butt, but it didn't faze Gabe Spooner.

"Don't get on your high horse with me, son. I've spanked your ass and wiped your nose before you was weaned. I said I can read men pretty good — and that includes you. I've had to listen to a lot of your lies over the years . . . "

"Back off, Gabe!" snapped the Colonel. "You accusing Morg of something?"

Gabe faced the Hammers squarely. "Colonel, if Sundance was slugged stupid by Merry and Iliffe, how did he kill 'em?"

The elder Hammer frowned, turned to Morg.

"He come round and started shootin'!

Me and Mitch went in with guns blazing and he got Mitch . . . "

"You said you arrived after Mitch had been shot by Sundance," cut in Gabe and he saw the Colonel had also picked up the discrepancy in Morg's story. "You said you arrived as Sundance was shooting all three in the head."

There was silence and accusing stares and Morg's shoulders slumped. "Ah, hell — all right. I nailed them two old women. Mitch and me went after Sundance but he winged me and downed Mitch — I — put a bullet in the heads of all three after Sundance lit out for the hills. I had this plan of blamin' him for the murders like I told you . . . "

Gabe's mouth tightened and the Colonel turned to his ramrod slowly. "Like I said, the boy was thinking, and it doesn't change a thing — we make sure Sundance is shot dead and that's it. Keystone dies with that Reb."

"You'll have to tell me about Keystone sometime, pa." Morg was mighty relieved to know his father was accepting his actions and Gabe shrugged, going along with the plan, too. After all, he was used to siding the Colonel.

"Some day," Hammer replied curtly. "Gabe, I'll ride in to town with Morg and front Ty Monroe. You go back to the ranch, get the men scouring those hills, and tell them there's two hundred in it for the man who nails Sundance — I want that son of a bitch dead before daybreak! Now, move!"

Gabe nodded and set his mount close to Colonel Hammer's and spoke softly into the man's ear.

"You've raised a killer, Colonel. You've raised yourself a real killer."

Then he spurred away, turning back towards the pass before Hammer could reply.

★ ★ ★

He had fallen at some time but didn't remember when. He had a vague recollection of tumbling out of the saddle in semi-darkness and then — nothing.

Sundance was shivering with cold when he came to, lying against a rock, his shoulder throbbing almost as much as his head, sticky with blood on one side. His horse nuzzled him. He grabbed at a foreleg and laboriously pulled himself up, leaning heavily against the animal, one hand clinging tightly to the saddlehorn. He fumbled the canteen to his lips, swilled out his mouth, then drank. He shuddered. The water was cold and he was still shivering.

He was surprised to find his warbag tied on behind the saddle and his numbing fingers plucked at the knots of the rawhide straps so he could get his jacket free. He shrugged into it, buttoned it across his chest and by then his legs had taken all they could. They buckled and he crawled in between two rocks and sat there, huddled against the wind.

He had no idea how long he stayed there, his mind a blank, his skull pounding rhythmically. His vision was a little better but he still felt kind of queasy.

He had trouble trying to hold his thoughts and thinking straight. He managed to roll and light a cigarette but it tasted foul and he jabbed it out against the boulder.

Something about explosions . . . Yeah! He'd been blasting stumps. Where? On Keystone? . . . No, of course not. Keystone was long gone, he could remember that much. Then where . . . ?

He was just arranging the swirling memories when he heard the riders, the creak of saddle leather, jingle of harness or spur rowels, low voices.

He crawled out of the rocks and found he was on a high piece of ground in what looked like foothills of a black range that rose above him against the stars. On the trail below, one that he could see writhed like a pale snake up the slope towards his position, he saw the bunch of riders. Must be nigh on twenty men, he reckoned.

Then two more riders came to join them from the other trail and he recognized the voice of one of the men: the Colonel.

"Nice timing, Gabe — now you men understand that the marshal wants Sundance taken alive if possible . . . " He winked.

"Not 'if possible', Colonel," broke in Ty Monroe. "I want him *alive* so's he can stand trial. I don't care if he's wounded, long as he can sit in a court room and hear a jury's verdict. Now is that clear . . . bring him in alive."

There were murmurs that could have meant anything and by then Sundance was trying to mount the chestnut, his boot slipping two or three times from the stirrup.

Gabe Spooner below heard the sound of his boot slapping the rock. "What's that? Someone's up there on Squaw's Leap!"

The posse surged forward and by then Sundance was in the saddle. Instinct made him slide the Winchester free of the saddle scabbard and as he started to turn the horse, he realized he was in a good position for defence here. The trail was steep and narrow where it came out and the riders could only come up one at a time, maybe two abreast if someone didn't mind taking a chance riding along the edge.

He heeled the chestnut over to the top of the trail, suddenly threw his rifle to his shoulder and raked the rocks above the dark blotch of the moving riders, bullets kicking dust and rock chips down onto their shoulders.

His eyesight was just about good enough to hit the mountainside, he figured, levering and triggering, scattering the men.

As the echoes of gunfire died away, he heard the men cursing and frightened horses whinnying, but by that time he was wheeling away and giving the chestnut its head up the sloping trail.

They would come fast now, he thought, fumbling to reload the rifle, dropping three cartridges. He damn well wasn't in any condition to take on these men — why they wanted him he didn't know, but they had sounded mighty grim, or that damn Cheyenne marshal had, leastways.

Best thing to do was get the hell out of here and figure things out once he was safe.

He topped the ridge and sent the chestnut recklessly down the far side, sliding on the slope, dust pluming behind. He heard yells above, twisted to see the riders lining up along the ridge. A ripple of ragged flashes showed an instant before lead rattled through the stand of naked aspens he was passing.

The men started after him, some whooping like Indians, others taking pot-shots at him.

Holding his rifle in his left hand, he crouched low in the saddle and as soon as the horse hit the bottom, jammed home his spurs. It snorted once to let him know it didn't care for such treatment but responded with a quick gathering of muscles and a stretching-out of the legs and neck, tail flying.

Lead zipped around him, clattering amongst the bare-branched trees, buzzing off rocks. His knees worked by instinct, weaving the mount between the tree trunks, leaping it over deadfalls, skidding around boulders that appeared suddenly and unexpectedly. He was sweating now and it stung his eyes. Sundance wiped them swiftly but his vision was still blurred.

And he didn't see the low branch, busy watching the ground ahead. It slammed into his chest and swept him off the saddle as if he had been lassoed and jerked backwards.

He grunted as the breath blasted out of him and he rolled several yards before being able to gain control of his movements. He squirmed behind a deadfall as the posse spread out and came in pounding, guns hammering. Monroe yelled to hold their fire, *damnit*!

But the men kept shooting and Sundance spun onto his belly, beaded quickly and brought down a rider, horse and all. They rolled in a thrashing heap, unseating two more men, and then the others swept around the melee and came charging in, still shooting.

Splinters flew into his face. He jerked back, half rising. Something whipped his hat from his head. Something else tugged at his thick jacket sleeve, turning him. A man leapt his mount over the deadfall, leaning out of the saddle, firing his rifle one-handed.

The slug drove into the deadfall and then a second horse lifted over his shelter and rammed the first one, knocking rider and mount to the ground.

The newcomer quit leather in a leap and launched himself at Sundance who tried to bring his rifle around. It snagged in a dead branch of the log and then Marshal Ty Monroe was upon him, kicking the rifle from his grip, stomping him flat and standing with one boot across his throat as he pointed a cocked pistol down at his head.

"Bat an eyelid and you're halfway to hell, feller!" Monroe panted, eyes wild.

Sundance was dazed, couldn't see properly or even breathe easily. He lifted his hands awkwardly and Monroe raised his face to the other riders reining down.

"If I didn't know better, Colonel, I'd think your men had orders to shoot to kill!"

Colonel Hammer, mouth tight, forced a little levity into his voice. "Hell, my men haven't seen action in years, marshal, guess they got a mite overexcited, that's all."

Monroe gave no sign at first that he accepted the rancher's explanation, but then he nodded jerkily, leaned down and fisted up the front of Sundance's shirt. He hauled the man roughly to his feet.

"Well, mister, you're in one piece just like I wanted you — you got anythin' to say before I lock you up?"

"I don't remember what happened . . ."

Monroe shook him. "You don't remember killin' three men and woundin' young Morg Hammer?"

Sundance frowned, aware of Morg now and the dark stain on the man's shirt.

"Sounds like a good story to me, Ty," scoffed Morg.

Monroe pursed his lips. "Maybe — but he's had a wallop across the head and there's blood . . . But we'll see. C'mon, Reb. Let's go."

As the marshal boosted the manacled Sundance up into the saddle, Colonel Hammer said quietly to Spooner, "You let me down, Gabe. Now the son of a bitch'll talk his head off once he remembers. He'll give 'em an earful about Keystone!"

"I told the men to shoot to kill, Colonel. Havin' Monroe along cramped their style — but mebbe we can put it right."

"You damn well better . . . "

Then Monroe, mounted now, said, "Thanks for your help, Colonel. I'll handle this now. Keep yourself and Morg available in case I want to question you. G'night."

Hammer swore softly as Monroe escorted Sundance away.

9

Break-out

SUNDANCE lay stretched out on the bunk in the cell, hands clasped behind his head, staring up through the darkness to where he knew the ceiling to be.

It was too black for him to actually see it, but his gaze wasn't really focused. He was thinking, thinking hard, trying to recall what the hell had happened out there near the foothills when he had been blasting those stumps.

He thought he just about had it. Trouble with the second stump, needed a further charge. Someone coming up behind him and as he turned — *wham*! A mountain had fallen on him — although he had had a glimpse of two vague shapes.

Nothing then until — until — Hell

almighty, it was so vague! Like a dream . . .

Gunfire. Two men shooting at him and he shot back instinctively. Hit one. Got the second, too, and the first dived over rocks and . . . two other men sprawled in the dust . . .

Morg Hammer!

The name blasted into his head out of nowhere. Yeah, Morg Hammer and the other hombre he had downed and who was writhing and yelling was Mitch O'Reilly, the one he'd shot just after he'd quit the Hammer spread . . .

Self-preservation must have made him mount his horse and run for it. Then the goddamn posse! Doing their best to kill him . . . the hostility of the marshal . . . and jail . . .

Knowing did nothing to relax him. He tried to get some sleep but saw the cell gradually lighten from grey to amber to the dimness that would pass for full daylight in this place with its stone walls and small, high windows.

Monroe brought him a breakfast

tray, coffee, greasy bacon, a slab of stale bread with granular home-churn butter.

"You feelin' better or you want the doc again?"

"Again?" asked Sundance, and then vaguely recalled a man bending over him by lamp light. He touched his head. "That's who bandaged my head . . . I'm okay, marshal."

"Remember yet?" The lawman sounded sceptical and showed his surprise when Sundance said, yeah, he recollected most of what happened.

Then, at Monroe's insistence, he told his story while he ate. The marshal had smoked down a cigarette while listening, handed tobacco sack and papers through the bars when Sundance had finished.

"Some different to the way Morg Hammer tells it." And he told Sundance what Morg claimed to have happened.

"I never shot any man in the back of the head, dying or otherwise, marshal — and I tell you, Mitch was alive,

172

though bad-hit, I reckon, as I recall it. Think Iliffe might've yelled out, too . . . "

"Judas, man, you're layin' a lot on young Morg! I always figured him to have a killer streak, but what the hell could he gain by telling this kinda story about you?"

Sundance accepted a vesta, fired up his cigarette and exhaled smoke through the bars. "That posse seemed keen to shoot me out from under my hat last night, marshal . . . I don't reckon I was meant to see the inside of any jail. Only the inside of a pine box."

Monroe said nothing for a spell, then spoke quietly. "Same impression I had. But I insisted they bring you in alive and I did get there before Hammer's men had a chance to hunt for you . . . Why would the Colonel want you dead, Sundance?"

"S'pose you're gonna put me on trial?"

Monroe frowned. "Might come to

that. Depends on what I find out — I'll need to question Morg again — Why?"

"Well, marshal, if I'm to have my day in court, I aim to make the most of it. You just see the court's packed with townsfolk. Maybe they'll learn something mighty interesting about their war hero Colonel Hammer."

The lawman's face darkened. "Now, listen, mister, if you think you're gonna use me because of some vendetta you got goin' with the Colonel . . . "

Sundance wandered back to his bunk, sat down on the edge, then swung up his legs, stretching out and blowing smoke at the ceiling. The casualness of it made Monroe mad.

"Goddamn Reb! You're all the same . . . Just won't give in, will you? Just won't accept that we whipped you and we'll do it again every time you try to go up agin us!"

"Marshal, I never killed Bill Merry or Iliffe. I think I shot Mitch O'Reilly, but he was still alive, far as I recollect when

I lit out . . . You've got the wrong man behind bars."

"That so? Then how come you can be sure it didn't happen the way Morg said? You were sufferin' concussion, accordin' to the sawbones. He said it'd affect your memory."

"Mebbe — but now I've got my memory back. I reckon it was a way of nailing me without the Colonel appearing to be personally involved."

"You're loco. I think I can see it now, you got such a goddamn hate on for the Colonel that . . . "

"Go to hell, Monroe," cut in Sundance, suddenly weary of it all. "You've made up your mind, I can see that. But you just remember what I said — when you get me to court."

Monroe heeled abruptly, almost tripped over the breakfast tray, kicked it angrily along the passage, and then stomped out of the cell block.

Sundance lay there in the coolness of the cell, drawing his jacket across his chest as he smoked silently.

Well, that ought to stir something up, he figured . . .

Only problem was, he was still locked up and as long as he was, they had him hog-tied.

★ ★ ★

Rachel Hammer looked pale but determined as she made her way down the stairs and into the dining room where her father and Morg were eating breakfast.

"Help your sister to the table," the Colonel said curtly to Morg who rose languidly and did no more than hold out a chair for Rachel.

She sank down gratefully, gave her surly brother a quick on-off smile and waited while Peaches brought her flapjacks and coffee.

"You still look piqued," Hammer remarked. "Why didn't you have Peaches bring your breakfast up to you?"

"I'm getting stronger by moving around, father, thank you . . . " She glanced at Morg and then at her father. "Morg told me earlier about all the excitement yesterday and last night . . . That Texan or whatever he is is lucky to be alive."

"Damn right he is," growled Morg. "And if I had my way . . . "

"Watch your language at my table, boy," cut in the Colonel, studying his daughter, recognizing criticism in her tone. "But Morg's right — that Reb could've been shot down. My God, a triple murderer! Most of the boys feel that a rope on the spot is the only answer for a man like that. Can't blame them. After all, Mitch was their bunk-mate."

"Damn — you bet, pa," Morg agreed.

The girl toyed with her flapjacks, looking down at her plate. "I can't believe it. Oh, I know you say I hardly know the man but I like to think I'm a good judge of character and I'm sure he's not the cold-blooded killer everyone makes out."

"Listen, sis, if you're calling me a liar . . . !"

"Enough! It happened the way Morg told it — can you give any other explanation than cold-blooded murder for what Sundance did, Rachel?"

"No-ooo — Not if it happened the way Morg said, I can't."

"There you go again, doubtin' my word!"

Before she could reply, Gabe Spooner appeared in the doorway, looking tight-lipped.

"Marshal's ridin' in, Colonel."

Hammer ripped off his napkin and hurled it onto the table. "All right — we'd best offer him breakfast, I suppose — bring him in. Rachel, you go back to your room."

"Oh, father, can't I stay? I'm fed up with that stuffy old room."

"Do like I say, girl. Peaches will bring your meal."

Sighing, knowing it was no use arguing, Rachel stood a little shakily and moved slowly from the room. She smiled briefly at Gabe and Ty Monroe as they entered. Peaches was waiting to help her up the stairs.

Monroe said he'd just have coffee and the Colonel poured him a cup. Gabe sat down, rolling a cigarette, waiting. Morg looked tense.

"Sundance tells a different story," Monroe announced.

The Colonel scoffed. "Well, of course he would! Did you expect a confession, Ty?"

"Mebbe not — but accordin to the doc, he had concussion and it affected his memory. Now he reckons he can remember pretty good and his story don't hardly resemble Morg's . . . "

He looked bleakly at the young rancher and Morg tried to remain calm, curled a lip. "So he's a liar as well as a triple murderer. It don't surprise me none, marshal."

"Just how did his story go?" Gabe Spooner asked quietly and they all glanced at him before Monroe spoke.

"Said he come to and Iliffe and

179

Merry were already down, Iliffe moanin'. Mitch and Morg were comin' at him with guns . . . "

"Oh, yeah!" scoffed Morg.

"He admits shootin' Mitch and wingin' you, then makin' a run for it when you dodged behind some rocks. He says Mitch was still alive, though bad hit, when he pulled out."

The three J-Link-H men kept their faces carefully blank.

"Like I said, man's a goddamn liar," Morg growled. "I ain't sure where Merry and Iliffe fit in except he was s'posed to've beat up on' em accordin' to Kit Dunson, so maybe they was gonna square things with him — that's guess-work. But I do know Mitch was on the prod for him and he was on his face, shot in the back of the head when I arrived, and Sundance was giving the finishing shots to the other two — I admit I was scared but I never got a chance to do much before he spotted me and winged me . . . Sure, I ran. Wouldn't you? Three dead men and

the man who did it still there shootin'
at you?"

"Morg's story sounds the most
logical to me, Ty," the Colonel said
carefully.

"I had more to do with Sundance
than anyone else here," Gabe Spooner
said, " . . . and I was sure worried
I'd brought him back to the spread.
Few things he said made me think he
was a killer . . . I told the Colonel I'd
made a mistake bringing him back but
the Colonel bein' the kinda man he is,
said he saved Miss Rachel so he was
entitled to a chance — now look what's
happened. Three men dead and he's
tryin' to pin it on Morg. Who he took
an instant dislike to, I might add."

Monroe seemed as if he could easily
savvy that but refrained from saying so
aloud. "Then you're stickin' by your
story, Morg?"

"Why the hell wouldn't I? It's what
happened."

"Look, Ty, I understand you have
to investigate but, God almighty, man,

you must know this Sundance is a violent man! He not only fought with Morg in the canyon, he gunwhipped him and threatened my men if they pulled any more cowboy hi-jinks he'd start shooting back by way of reply — and he was well to the fore in that big brawl in town and claims he argued with his trail boss and quit. My guess is the trail boss fired him."

Monroe was frowning, sipping his coffee, noncommittal.

"Why don't you ask Kit Dunson if he did beat up on her men?" Spooner suggested.

"That's what I aim to do. Way things look now, it'll have to go to trial." Monroe swung his gaze to the Colonel's face as he spoke and saw the flare of alarm briefly in the man's eyes before Hammer composed himself.

"Fairest way all round, I suppose," the Colonel said curtly. "But I resent Morg's word being doubted, Ty."

"Just doin' my job, Colonel. I'm impartial in this. I'm content to let the court decide . . . and you go along with that, I reckon."

"As I said, fairest way . . . "

The marshal left as soon as he had drained his coffee and Colonel Hammer swore as the door closed behind him.

"By God, this is one hell of a mess, Morg!"

"Wouldn't've been if we'd been able to nail Sundance last night."

"But we didn't, damnit! Forget the 'what ifs' and 'buts'. We've got us a pack of trouble coming up if Sundance reaches that court room."

Gabe Spooner, coming from seeing the marshal off, heard the words. "What we need now is for Sundance to be shot while trying to escape."

Colonel Hammer sat down again, looking thoughtful, waved his son and foreman to their chairs. "Yes — let's do some thinking along those lines . . . "

Half an hour later he called Peaches and told her to bring Rachel downstairs and when the girl arrived he smiled, held a chair for her and said, "Rachel, I'm giving the boys a night on the town — Morg and I are riding in. I was thinking a ride might do you some good. In the buckboard, of course, so you can stretch out in the back should you feel faint — would you like to come? Perhaps you could visit this Sundance and hear for yourself just what he has to say . . . I mean, fair's fair . . . "

"Oh, father, I'd love that."

"Good — oh, the marshal seems convinced he's guilty and he says the town's very riled and there's some talk of lynching . . . I thought if we had our men on hand we might be able to head it off. Whatever he's done, we owe Sundance a lot. He's entitled to a fair trial. No man should be lynched out of hand . . . "

The girl looked paler than ever at mention of such an incident.

"Wouldn't surprise me none if he tried to break out once he got wind of a lynch mob," Spooner said. "Not that you could blame him — I sure wouldn't want to stick around."

"Yeah," Morg said flatly. "But he'd never do it alone."

Rachel looked from one man to the other, stood up, holding to the back of the chair. "Well, I'll go get ready, father . . ."

"Have Peaches help you dress," the Colonel said, frowning as she left. "I'm not easy at using her this way, Gabe . . ."

"Well, she's the one person Monroe'll never suspect," Spooner said and the Colonel nodded resignedly.

Morg took out his Peacemaker and began checking the loads

★ ★ ★

Kit Dunson quickly threw the tarp over the box of dynamite in the barn as she saw Marshal Ty Monroe dismounting in the yard. She walked slowly to the doorway and waved, waiting for him to come to her.

185

"Mornin', Kit — gonna be warm if that wind don't get up."

"I expect it'll be blowing after noon, Ty. You're a stranger. Come up to the house and we'll have coffee." As they started walking towards the house she asked casually, "Is this an official visit . . . ?"

"Yeah, I s'pose it is. Wanted to ask you about Sundance and Merry and Iliffe — I heard he beat up on them."

Kit paused on the porch. "They had something of a 'difficulty' — just how bad it was, I'm not sure . . ."

"We got that Reb locked up in jail, by the way."

"From what I hear that's the best place for him . . ."

She was pleasant enough as she prepared the coffee but inwardly she was seething. Now she wouldn't be able to go anywhere near Hellfire Pass. Her plan would have to be postponed.

Unless Sundance was turned loose, of course — or escaped.

***

The journey to town exhausted Rachel and the Colonel insisted she retire to the suite of rooms that he kept at the Cheyenne Hotel on a permanent basis.

"You rest up this afternoon and you can visit Sundance this evening if you want . . . Take him his supper, maybe."

She smiled at her father's suggestion, insisted she did not need the doctor's attentions, and said she would rest the whole afternoon.

That suited the Colonel and he hurried downstairs to where Gabe and Morg waited in the hotel foyer.

"All right, give the men two dollars each to get them started. As soon as it's dark we'll buy them a few drinks to make it look good — you have some known trouble-makers picked out, Gabe?"

"Sure. Hank Longtree and Tiny Swift. They're always spoilin' for a fight. And I seen Garth Tyson in town, too. If he stays over, a nester'll be the best excuse of all . . . "

Hammer nodded, glanced at Morg. "The other taken care of?"

"Yeah, pa. I'd like to be one of 'em myself . . . "

"No! No, you stay where you can be seen, like the rest of us . . . As long as the men you've picked are trustworthy."

"As much as fifty bucks will buy," Morg said with a scowl.

"Then that's all we can do — for now. All right, go about your business. We meet in the bar of the *Belle*, OK, soon as the sun goes down . . . And for God's sake make sure nothing happens to Rachel!"

★ ★ ★

Marshal Ty Monroe was surprised when Rachel Hammer entered his office, the last of the sundown fire in the street behind her. When she

188

stepped into the lamp's light he saw how pale and drawn she was and immediately offered her a chair but she refused.

Then he saw there was someone with her. He recognized Foster Neeley, son of the diner's owner, and the young gawky man was holding a tray covered with a white napkin.

"I thought I'd bring Sundance a decent meal, marshal, instead of you going to the trouble of cooking him something. In fact, there's a plate of stew and some apple pie for you, too." Rachel's smile was irresistible.

Monroe salivated at the thought of a decently cooked meal and, of course, could hardly refuse to allow the girl to take the food in to the prisoner.

Rachel uncovered the tray while Foster Neeley held it, looking a mite fussed in her presence. She set the plates and cutlery on the marshal's desk and the sight of the food melted the very last of any resistance he might have still retained.

He sat down, staring at the savoury-smelling steam as it wafted towards his face.

"All right, Rachel. You best go on ahead and feed Sundance. Tell him he don't know how lucky he is . . . "

"I'd like to stay and visit him for a short while, marshal. Whatever he's done, he did save my life . . . "

"Long as you like," Monroe said, unable to refrain any longer from starting to eat the big plate of stew.

Rachel and Foster Neeley went into the passage leading to the cell block and the lawman didn't even notice the diner man leaving. He had gravy dripping from his chin as he mopped at his plate with a thick hunk of corn-pone and couldn't wait to start on the big wedge of apple pie . . .

Sundance sat on his bunk with the tray balanced on his knees, looking at the girl as he ate.

"You recovering all right, Rachel?"

"Slowly — I hate to be incapacitated and perhaps I push a little harder than

I should, but I hope to be riding within a day or two."

"Well, don't push it too hard — you've got plenty of time and 'easy does it' is best. It was mighty nice of you to bring me a decent meal. Ty Monroe might be a good lawman but as a cook . . . " He smiled as he shook his head and the girl smiled in return.

She fiddled with her handbag in her lap. "I'm sorry for the trouble you're in. It seems Morg's the cause of it — I mean, because of the story he told."

He sensed she was asking him if it was true or not and he shook his head. "It didn't happen that way. Not as I recollect it, leastways, but I guess any lawyer worth his salt will soon hang his hat on the fact I had concussion and couldn't be sure what had happened. In which case, it might keep them from hanging me, but not from sending me to prison for a long, long time."

"It's an awful situation you're in." She paused, plucking away at her handbag. She glanced down the dim passage to where there was a glow coming from the front office and lowered her voice. "I suppose you'd rather be out of here . . . "

He paused, chewing the last of the meat in the stew, looking through the bars at her. He couldn't see her very well despite the wall lamp's light.

"I sure would . . . But if I do get as far as the court . . . " He stopped, picking up some bread and breaking off a hunk to mop at the gravy. Don't be a fool, he told himself. *No sense in telling her how you aim to smash her father's reputation once they get you into that court room . . . She'll be shocked and hurt enough when it happens . . .*

"Yes?" she asked, expectantly.

"What, Rachel?"

"I — had the impression you were going to say something more . . . "

"Oh? I disremember. That was a fine stew and you tell it to whoever made it . . . What's that?"

There were the sound of shouting and a sudden shattering of glass, then more shouting. Rachel's hand went to her bruised throat.

"Oh, dear God! The lynch mob!"

Sundance stiffened. "Lynch party?"

She was on her feet now, gripping the bars. "I — there's supposed to be some men who want to — lynch — you . . . "

Then they heard a man yelling in the front office.

"Marshal, you better get over to the *Belle*, pronto! There's one helluva brawl startin' and someone's gonna get killed if you don't stop it!"

They heard the lawman's chair fall with a clatter as he jumped to his feet. There was a pause, likely as he grabbed his guns, and then he called briefly down the passage before going out onto the street, "Stay put, Rachel! Lock this front door after me and don't let no one back in but me, hear?"

"Yes, marshal!"

Pale, she hurried as fast as she could

down the passage, one hand touching the walls now and again so as to help her keep her balance. She fumbled with the bolts and bar on the door.

By now Sundance was at the bars, gripping them with both hands.

He could hear the sounds from outside, ugly sounds, sounds that carried the hint of death with them . . .

Then Rachel, somewhat breathless, came back down the passage. She paused a few feet from the door, then brought her hand out from behind her back.

She was holding the ring of cell keys.

10

Hell-for-Leather

HANK LONGTREE started it. It was easy, seeing as that fool nester, Garth Tyson, came into the bar, trailed by his cousin who worked for him and was an even bigger fool than Tyson himself.

The cousin turned grey and halted just inside the batwings when he saw the room was crammed with cattlemen. He tugged at Tyson's sleeve.

"Garth — man, we don't b'long in here! Let's go. I can do without a drink."

Tyson was startled and not a little uneasy, too, at seeing so many cattlemen in town this night. Usually they came on a Saturday . . . But he was a stubborn man, heavy-muscled from work on the land but slow, too.

"I want a drink, Mel," he said, forcing himself to speak loud enough so he could be heard above the din in the bar. "And I aim to have it." He reached out for Mel's coat and tugged him forward. "C'mon, I'll buy you one, too."

The cowmen watched, opened out for him to reach the bar and both nesters felt a sense of relief: it was going to be all right after all. They weren't going to make trouble . . .

Bellying up to the bar, Garth Tyson reached into his pocket for a coin and said to the bar keep, "Two whiskies' Hal — I'm buyin'."

Big Hank Longtree, hunched over an almost empty beer glass, straightened slowly, and when the 'keep brought the whiskies, held out his now empty glass.

"What's this?" the barman said warily.

"Fill 'er up, Hal. You heard Tyson — he's buyin', he said so."

The 'keep stepped back, licking his

lips as he glanced at the startled homesteader.

"Aw, now, Hank, I meant I was buyin' for Mel here, not the whole bar!"

Longtree, straightfaced, towered over Tyson although the latter was wider through the shoulders. "You sayin' you ain't gonna buy me a drink?"

"That's right. I don't have enough money for one thing and, like I said, I was buyin' just for Mel here."

Longtree looked around as the cowmen started to close in. "Now, that's a damn insult if ever I heard one . . . A stinkin' nester straight-out refusin' to buy a broke cowpoke a drink . . ."

That was it. There was only one way it could go from there and both Tyson and Mel knew they had walked into a trap and all they could do was hope they could fight their way out of it.

Longtree provoked Tyson into taking the first swing and then the whole room seemed to explode in violence. Tiny

Swift — a tall man who did not live up to his nickname — picked up a chair and hurled it through the bar mirror. A townsman objected as Swift had known he would, and had his nose smashed almost to the back of his head.

Other cowmen turned on the townsmen nearest them and fists flailed and boots lashed out, furniture splintered and glass shattered as men yelled wildly.

Colonel Hammer and Gabe and Morg had arrived just a fraction late. The plan had been for him to buy rounds of drink until the men appeared drunk and out of control, but Garth Tyson appearing in the midst of the cowmen had precipitated the action.

The three men stood to one side and watched as Marshal Ty Monroe came charging in, shooting off his six-gun into the ceiling, but the gunfire had no effect whatsoever. The men kept on brawling and the lawman waded in, swinging his gun barrel indiscriminately, brave and maybe foolhardy . . .

The Colonel nodded to the eager Morgan. He spoke crisply. "All right. Get your men into position and then start 'helping' Monroe — it's important that we be seen to be doing our best to break this up. Now hurry!"

Morg spun away, shouldering into the edge of the brawling men. He touched a redhead on the shoulder, dodged the punch the man automatically threw as he came around and thrust him out of the fight.

"Watch what the hell you're doin', Red! Find Early and get yourselves into position."

The big redhead nodded, lowering his fists sheepishly. "Sorry, Morg . . . "

He flung himself into the fight and moments later, accompanied by a black-bearded man with an eyepatch and one ear torn where it joined his head, hurried to the side door where Morg waited, holding it partly open.

"Move it. You collect your fifty each afterward. Back here."

The men went out and Morg turned, nodded to his father on the fringe of the fighting and then pushed into the melee, using knee and fists, finally drawing his gun and striking out left and right.

Enjoying himself.

Gabe Spooner worked his way up alongside the sweating, bleeding marshal, jostled the man to make sure he was seen and then started trying to break up the shouting, punching, biting, kicking men.

By now the saloon was a shambles and the brawl was overflowing into the street through shattered batwings, involving onlookers on the boardwalk.

Good, thought Colonel Hammer, grabbing a man by the back of the neck and smashing his face into the edge of the bar. The bigger the better, and the more noise to help drown the gunfire, the happier he'd be.

★ ★ ★

"You'll have to hurry!" Rachel Hammer said with a plea in her voice as Sundance strode into the front law office. "I have the key to the rear door here . . . You're going the wrong way!"

"Got to pick up my guns," he threw back over his shoulder, looking around swiftly. He saw the locked cabinet on the wall and figured the marshal's weaponry was in there, as well as any guns taken from the prisoners.

There was no time to waste searching for the padlock's key. He snatched a heavy-bladed Bowie knife from a sheath dangling from the hat pegs, got it behind the hasp and levered brutally, forcing the screws out of the stained wood. Inside were a row of rifles, two shotguns and several pistols and, on the floor of the cupboard, his own gunrig and Smith and Wesson.

He buckled it on quickly, snatched his own rifle from the clips and turned to the pale-faced girl leaning against the door frame, looking nervous and anxious.

Sundance crossed to her in two strides, took her shoulders between his big hands. "Rachel — you're going to be in trouble for doing this . . . "

"I . . . I'll be all right. I have father to stand up for me."

"Maybe he won't after you helping me escape."

"It was he — and Gabe, too — who put the notion into my head in the first place. They said they wouldn't blame any man trying to escape from a lynch mob. That — anyone — was entitled to a fair trial."

Sundance stiffened, eyes narrowed: then he took her arm and led her to the rear door. He took the key ring from her and tried the keys one by one.

"You have to come back, you understand that, don't you?"

He frowned over his shoulder. "Come back?"

"For the trial. You have to clear your name and the only way is at a fair trial."

He had his own notions about just

202

how 'fair' a trial he'd get. And he couldn't believe how naïve this young girl was. It was endearing but . . . He nodded soberly and said, "You're right. I guess a trial is the only way."

She stepped close and he felt her hand go into his jacket pocket. "Read it when you get a chance. It may help."

Still none the wiser, Sundance nodded, returned to searching for the right door key. "I'm going to the livery for my horse. You wait until I clear the yard, then go back to your hotel." At last the door opened under his hands.

"But I want to see you away safely! You saved *my* life and I want to return the favour."

"You did that by opening the cell door. Thanks again. *Adios*, Rachel."

He slipped out into the night and the first thing he did was lever a shell into the breech of the rifle.

Keeping the dark of the greystone building at his back, he made his way across the yard. The brawl sounded very loud from out here and there were several scattered gunshots. His mouth tightened.

They'd planned it carefully. Any gunfire would be considered as part of or the results of the riot . . . His body likely wouldn't be found until long after the trouble had been quelled. His mouth tightened at the thought of how the Colonel had used the girl — his own daughter. Well, that was just something else to square away when the time came.

Providing he survived this night . . .

He made his way to the paling fence through tangled weeds and junk. Tensed, mouth dry. Nothing happened. Gripping the rifle tightly he moved towards the gate but almost there found some loose palings. Two of them moved easily and gave him enough room to slip out into the dark alley beyond. He sensed danger.

On Main, timber splintered and more glass shattered. The odd gunshot punctuated the night, already rowdy with the shouts and yells of innocents caught up in the riot. Looking left he glimpsed some of the struggling, running figures on Main, flattened himself against the fence as a man dodged into the alley followed by two others, cursing. They pounded past him without a glance and he started forward, but froze when two gunshots sounded from his right — the way the running man had gone.

Snapping his head around, he could just make out the dark shapes of men down there. The two pursuers had stopped in frozen motions, as if uncertain what to do next. One man even had his hands half-raised. The man they had been chasing seemed to be down and as Sundance watched he began writhing about and moaning in the dust and the two pursuers, suddenly sobered, turned and started running back towards him.

Neither held a gun. Then he saw a fourth shadow step out from behind a tree on the other side of the lane, the man quickly kneeling beside the downed townsman.

Sundance soon figured the kneeling man had been waiting in ambush for him, had mistaken the ranny fleeing the brawl for his target.

He heard the man curse, saw his head snap up. He must have seen Sundance against the light glow, brought up his pistol, hurling himself forward full-length as he fired. Sundance heard the whip of the bullet past his head, dropped to one knee, shooting the rifle from the hip. The killer rolled into the darkness at the base of the fence, snapping two fast shots as he did so.

Sundance threw himself against the fence, hearing the palings rattle, dropped flat and, as the killer triggered again, fired his rifle along the base of the fence, only inches above the ground.

The man grunted and swore and as Sundance levered in another cartridge he saw him lurch to his feet, fighting to keep his balance, one hand pressed into his midriff. Sundance put his second shot into him and the man spun violently, going down in that awkward way he had seen the enemy fall so often during the war — the way that told him the man was dead before he hit the ground.

He ran forward, rifle reloaded, knelt swiftly. The killer was lying on his back, his chest blown open, mouth slack, a patch over one eye.

"Early!" Sundance breathed, recognizing the man from J-Link-H. He turned to the wounded man. "You OK, feller?"

The man nodded. "Hey — was layin' *for* — you! You best — git!"

He got out of there fast in case someone realized where the shooting had come from and that there had been rifle fire mixed in with the pistol shots.

As he quit the alley he threw one last look over his shoulder and saw a small bunch of men charging into the lane, guns drawn.

His time was running out . . .

He came into the livery stables

through the corral area, talking in a low voice to the nervous mounts as he worked his way through them. The marshal had told him his chestnut was stabled here and that Sundance would have to pay any charges due. *Sure — if he lived long enough!*

Crouched beside a post, rifle at the ready, he was half listening to the sounds of what seemed to have become a riot now, and strained to see into the darkness of the livery.

Hammer's second man was bound to be waiting in there . . .

His hat was hanging down his back by the throat thong, having fallen there during his rush from the laneway. Now he crouched and entered the stables, swiftly moving away from the open archway and into the shadows. Almost instantly a gun bellowed and the bullet smacked into the plank wall beside his head. Splinters stung his cheek and neck. He rolled and two more bullets kicked straw and dirt from the ground. Sundance launched himself into the first stall and this time a shotgun thundered and a large piece of the partition was chewed out. He swore, brushed some slivers of wood off his shoulder and head — then realized the white bandage was likely giving the killer something to shoot at. He tore off the bandages, clawed up a handful of dirt and dropped it into the cloth circle. He fired the Smith and Wesson three times, aiming in the general direction of the killer, tossed the weighted bandage with his left into the next stall. After the last shot, he kicked the planks and grunted as if he had vaulted the partition.

He glanced up at the loft and there was movement up there. A dark shadow rose like a man on one knee and a stray reflection of light danced along the twin barrels of the shotgun.

Sundance launched himself into the aisle, levering and triggering the rifle, barrel angled upwards. Splinters flew and straw erupted in a swirling funnel. The shotgun blasted wildly out to one side and the man lifted halfway to his feet, struggled to keep his balance, and then plunged down into the aisle.

Sundance was moving before the man's body struck the ground. Several stalled mounts were whinnying and tugging at their tethers because of the shooting. His ears were ringing and he couldn't tell if the brawl was still going on or not. Fourth stall along he found the chestnut, threw his saddle on and cinched up swiftly. He slid a boot into the stirrup, clinging to the horn, hanging on one side of the horse as he urged it down the aisle.

Men burst in from Main, yelling. Someone started shooting and other guns joined in. Bullets whistled overhead, thudded into the plank walls. Two men appeared in the rear archway as he swung his leg over the chestnut's back, lay low and urged it on. He swerved the horse at the men and one man got off a shot that burned across his back and shoulders, knocking him halfway out of the saddle. Then the horse struck the man, his body hurtling as if shot from a catapult into the arch post. He fell silently while the other man was rolling frantically through the straw and manure in an effort to avoid being trampled.

The chestnut burst into the night and Sundance thrust out his arm behind him, emptying his pistol blindly, hoping the bullets would make the men keep their heads down.

Then he was skirting the corrals and the horse almost fell as it skidded around a corner, down an alley so narrow his boots actually scraped the walls of the buildings either side, and then across a weed-grown lot piled with garbage and junk and abandoned furniture, and, finally, into open country.

He dug in the spurs, beginning to feel the pain of the bullet wound in his back, the blood flooding down to his waistband now.

He fumbled to reload the pistol, decided to leave the rifle in its scabbard and fill its magazine when a better chance offered.

A glance over his shoulder showed men on horseback gathering outside the livery and then the night swallowed him up as he headed hell-for-leather towards the distant Storm Creek Range.

11

Hell at Hellfire

MARSHAL TY MONROE hadn't come out of the brawl too well — something of an understatement. He was a tough little rooster and enforced his own brand of law with gun barrel and fists when he had to. He was more feared than popular in Cheyenne.

So, during the brawl, many men — townsmen, nesters and cowboys alike — had taken the opportunity to get in a sly blow whenever the chance offered. Monroe had two cracked ribs, a foot so swollen from being stomped on that the doctor had had to cut the boot off, a busted nose, a badly cut eye that might affect his vision permanently, plus numerous cuts and abrasions. The medic insisted that the lawman spend a few days in his infirmary but Monroe was anxious to get back to his duties.

He was far from happy when the doctor told him that Sundance had escaped.

"Left two dead men and some more wounded or beaten. Will Overholser from the feed-and-grain store was shot in the alley behind the jail by Sid Early — who apparently mistook him for Sundance."

"What!"

"Red Haines was laying for Sundance in the livery, too, and he was shot dead."

The marshal squirmed, face clouded with anger. "Get the Colonel in here — and tell him to bring Rachel with him."

The doctor was too busy to be running errands for the law but he sent someone to find Hammer. When the man arrived, with the pale Rachel in tow, Monroe started in right off, virtually accusing him of arranging Sundance's escape.

Hammer looked wide-eyed innocent and not a little hurt. "Ty, I was right alongside you in the saloon!"

The marshal flicked his angry gaze to the girl and she lowered her eyes. "Yes, marshal, I let Sundance go free." She added quickly, "But he'll be back as soon as things quieten down." The lawman scoffed and she said, indignantly, "He *will*! He gave me his word — I only did it because I was afraid the mob would break in and try to lynch him."

Monroe turned to the Colonel. "Talkin' about lynchin' parties — don't believe I even seen a sign of one. Just a damn big riot." Hammer kept a puzzled look on his face as if he didn't understand and the marshal smothered a curse. "Two of your men were layin' for Sundance, Colonel."

The girl gasped and Hammer's face was suddenly hard and resentful. "I'm not responsible for what my men do when they've got a bellyful of booze, Monroe! Damnit, if they were smart enough to figure Sundance might try a jailbreak, I'd say that was to their credit."

Monroe's hands fisted up the sheets. He took a few moments to steady himself. "Ah, Colonel, I'm a mite too old and beat-up for this right now, and you always were better'n me with words . . . We'll just leave it, but I'll be getting back to you."

"While Sundance is running wild or clearing the territory!" Colonel Hammer shook his head vigorously. "Oh, no, marshal. The man's a killer and he has to be stopped. I'll organize my own posse."

"No, by Godfrey you won't! Here, Colonel! You come back! I don't want your men shooting Sundance on sight!"

But Hammer hurried the startled girl out of the infirmary and she pulled free, turned to him and asked sharply,

"Father, did you plant the idea of my releasing Sundance just so Early and Haines could shoot him down? While trying to escape?"

"Of course not! If they set up an ambush, it was their own doing. And never take that tone with me again, girl. You go on back to the ranch. I'll send Morg with you. I have a posse to organize."

"But the marshal said he doesn't want you to . . . "

"The hell with what Monroe wants. He's made a mess of this whole deal. I'm handling it personally from here on in — *And* I'll get results. You can depend on that!"

★ ★ ★

Sundance found that the girl had pushed a hand-drawn map into his jacket pocket at the back door of the jailhouse. It showed a trail leading from town deep into the hills before swinging out towards Hellfire Pass.

There was another, obviously very narrow, leading into what appeared to be a small box canyon. There was a big overhang of rock marked on the west side and the girl had written in a small neat hand: *Almost like a cave. Wait there. I'll come as soon as I can. R.*

He hadn't been expecting that. But he found the narrow trail leading in off the north end of the canyon, closest to Cheyenne. It led him upwards, the weary chestnut climbing slowly. Then the trail levelled out and he thought he had come to a dead end. But it had just narrowed way down so there was barely enough room for a man to ride through without touching the walls.

He easily found the rock overhang. It had been scoured so deeply by winds that had blown for hundreds of years that it was indeed almost a cave.

There were faint pictographs of tall, thin people and animals with stick-like legs. He recognized buffalo, deer, antelope, bighorn sheep and a mountain lion that, if true to scale, was much larger than any such lion in existence today.

He spread his bedroll and heated water in the skillet and twisted awkwardly as he tried to bathe the wound in his back. It was a long, curving shallow gouge that finished beneath his left shoulder as the bullet had angled upwards. He couldn't bandage it so wadded an undershirt over the area, pulled on his flannel shirt and buttoned his jacket tightly so as to hold it in place.

He was too tired to do anything else, even to make coffee. He slept with both guns unsheathed and against his body.

★ ★ ★

Rachel started up out of a deep sleep, alarmed at the grip on her shoulder. Her heart hammered but slowed when she saw Morg standing beside her bed, holding a leather-bound book.

"Wha — what's happened?" she asked anxiously and frowned when he thrust the book towards her.

"Somethin' for you to read."

Frowning, she sat up, pulling the

219

sheets across her. "Father's journal — how did you . . . ?"

"I found out a long time ago where he keeps the key to the safe. I was bored, so I got this out and read it . . . It'll open your eyes, sis. Our dear father ain't the gentleman hero he'd have us believe."

"Morgan, you've no right to this! It's private!"

"Not no more. But if you don't want to read it, give it back — hah! It ain't *that* private, eh? Take just a little peek . . . Go on. Guarantee you won't be able to close it up and hand it back to me after that . . . "

Rachel's mouth tightened. "All right — you make it sound so very intriguing. But we'll have to get it back in the safe before father returns."

"He won't be back for a couple of days. He aims to run down and kill that Reb this time . . . And damned if I'm going to stick around here while him and Gabe have all the fun."

"Morg — did you know anything

about a plan to have Sundance shot down while trying to escape? I think father might . . . "

He averted his eyes. "What's it matter? He was way too good for the idiots we — pa sent to set up the ambush. They reckon he's hit, though. Found blood in the stall where his horse was."

"Oh, dear God!"

"Ah, forget him, sis. He's just a Reb and he's out to destroy pa. He's *gotta* be hunted down or the Hammer name won't be worth a heap of goat's dung around here." He hitched at his gunbelt. "Put the book back as soon as you've finished with it."

"Morg, wait!" But he didn't answer, strode out, slamming the door behind him.

Slowly, Rachel pushed her hair back from her face and stared down at the heavy book she held for a long time. Then she opened it and began to read.

Martha Tyson had sent for Kit Dunson during the night to come and lend a hand with her husband Garth and his cousin Mel. She said they had been caught up in some sort of riot in Cheyenne. Although suffering from many wounds, neither man had stayed for attention by the doctor because the sawbones was run off his feet tending to so many injured men.

While Kit helped set Garth's broken arm and nose, extracted a broken tooth and then helped Martha sew up and bandage wounds, she learned about Sundance's violent escape and couldn't get away quick enough.

When she did get back to her place it was just about daybreak and she saw the posse pass by from town. There was enough light for her to be sure that most of the men were Hammer riders. They would be hunting Sundance in the hills — which suited her fine. It might be a little more risky but now she could put her plan into action.

She hurried into the house and went straight to her bedroom and the cedar chest that still contained some of her dead husband's clothes. She began to dress in shirt and trousers and although loose on her they would serve her purpose well enough.

A little later, as sunlight began to wash across the range, Kit Dunson headed for the hills, riding the only chestnut gelding in her remuda.

★ ★ ★

The box canyon was flooded with bright light when Sundance awoke, realizing he'd slept much later than he had meant to. Still a little groggy, he sat up and looked around, stiffened when he saw the rider coming across the canyon.

He recognized Rachel and waited for her to come up, feeling a mite foolish holding his rifle at the ready. She looked pale but waved him back when he started forward to help her dismount. "I'm all right. I've brought food and medicine."

After she had dressed his wound she said, "There is a posse looking for you but you're safe here. Peaches showed me this place years ago. She's a Cheyenne and said they used to hold ritual dances here but since they've mostly been herded onto reservations it's been in disuse for a long, long time."

His eyes searched her face. "Why're you helping me, Rachel? You don't owe me a thing."

"Except my life."

He waved that aside. "You've more than squared it by turning me loose."

She looked down at her hands. "I almost got you killed."

"I know you didn't know about the ambush . . . Look, Rachel, I don't like you getting involved in this any deeper — I — I have to go up against your father, and Morg, too, I guess. *Have* to. I can't explain right now, but . . . "

Tautly, she interrupted him. "About Keystone plantation, you mean?"

Sundance frowned. She was visibly upset, her voice choking with emotion, eyes filling.

"My father kept a journal. I — read it. I know all about what happened at Keystone."

He reached out, took her hands in his, looking down into that distraught face. "I'm sorry you had to find out like that — but you must see why I have to do what I'm planning."

"Can't you just ride on out? You don't have to go back now. I know a way out that can set you on a trail to the south in complete safety . . ."

He shook his head slowly. "They were my family, Rachel."

"But my father wasn't even *there*!"

"He's just as guilty as if he'd taken part in everything, Rachel," he told her quietly. "He gave the orders. He was a strict officer and wouldn't tolerate disobedience. His men did whatever he said, following orders to the letter."

"But he had *his* orders from General Sherman!" she protested, stamping her foot angrily. "The General said, 'Make the south suffer — teach it a lesson it'll never forget!'"

"Sure. And the interpretation was left to individual officers. There were plenty of atrocities because of that, maybe some worse than Keystone. But it was Keystone that affected me and I'm honour-bound to square things, Rachel."

She slumped, withdrew her hands from his grip. Twin lines of tears tracked down her windburned cheeks. "I was — hoping you'd see reason. Just this one time . . ."

"This one time is the only chance I'll get. I have to grab it with both hands."

"Then damn you!" She swayed, deathly white. "I won't let you kill my father, even though I've seen in his own handwriting what a — a monster he was. But he's still my father. And the war's been over for so long, Sundance!

My father's highly regarded up here. He's genuinely repentant about the war years . . . "

"When it suits him to appear so, Rachel. Look what he's doing to the nesters. He wants their land, hell or high water. He's bringing more and more pressure to bear, beating up crews and so on. Kit Dunson told me . . . "

"Kit Dunson is a trouble-maker!" Rachel snapped. "She and father used to be friendly but something happened between them and suddenly they were full of hate towards each other. True hate. She'll say and do anything to get back at him."

Sundance rolled a cigarette and lit up, watching the emotion tearing at her as she stood by her horse. She was a fine, decent young woman, and it hurt him to have to do this to her. But there could be no turning back: the Colonel and Gabe Spooner were doomed. Morg, too, if he threw his lot in with them. She was loyal to her father, of course, but she was compassionate, too, about Sundance's losses — and the circumstances of it must be tearing her apart, knowing the atrocities were carried out on her father's orders.

He spoke quietly. "Rachel, you'd best go."

She turned to mount without a word, but suddenly groped in her saddlebag and the new sun glinted off bright metal and he threw himself sideways as she fired. The bullet kicked gravel against his face as he rolled away and she fired again, thumbing the hammer awkwardly. The shot whined off the rock and the pistol jumped from her hand. Apparently she hadn't taken a firm enough grip and then he was confronting her, kicking the gun aside. She tried to fight him but was too weak and he easily lifted her into the saddle where she slumped, sobbing.

"I don't blame you, Rachel. I savvy you have to be loyal to the Colonel. You get on along home now. I'll quit this place and take my chances."

"Why can't you just — *go*! Please!"

He shook his head. He saw by her eyes that she knew it was the one thing he couldn't do for her. Then he unloaded her pistol, lifted the flap on the saddlebag to drop it in and saw the leather-bound book. He took out the journal and she tried to stop him but he stepped back out of reach.

"I think I'd better keep this, Rachel. Marshal Monroe might be interested in it."

"No! No, I have to put it back in father's safe!"

"Then why did you bring it? Hadn't quite made up your mind whether to show me or not, had you?"

She burst into tears, really sobbing, spitting words at him in a series of stutters. "I — hate — you — Sundance — Travis — or — whoever — you are! I — hate — you! I hope my father's — men — track — you — down and — and kill you!"

"They will if they get a chance, never

doubt it — sorry it's worked out this way, Rachel. I'm sorry for what it's done to you — and us."

"There's no 'us'!" Her mouth curled bitterly as she spoke. "Never will be — never. For a time I did think . . . "

Abruptly, she spurred away across the box canyon, leaving him standing holding the book and her empty pistol.

She was almost to the entrance when a man appeared there on foot, leading his horse, rifle in one hand.

It was Gabe Spooner and as soon as he spotted Sundance, he dropped his mount's reins and shouted at the girl.

"Get outta here, Rachel! I'll handle this!"

"No, Gabe! Wait!"

Spooner sprinted to her horse and whipped off his hat, and slapped it across the rump, Gabe's own mount veering away violently. He moved fast for an old man and Sundance was only just now hunting cover as the ramrod threw himself behind the nearest rocks, shooting wild as he launched his body across. The bullet ricocheted from the overhang, bringing down dust and chips onto Sundance's shoulders. He scooped up his own rifle, fired quickly and dropped behind a boulder.

Gabe Spooner was in good cover now, protected by a clump of boulders shoulder-high, and fired rapidly, lead raking Sundance's position. Then the foreman angled his gun upwards, shooting at the curved roof. The bullets spat downwards into the area occupied by Sundance's body.

He swore, put three fast shots into the foreman's shelter, and dived over the side of the overhang cave. He hit on his good shoulder, twisted, and slid down the slope. He hadn't reached the foot of the slope before Gabe raked it with a fast withering fire, Sundance twisting and rolling his body in an effort to dodge the hail of lead thudding all around him. Then he dug in his heels, gritting his teeth as the sudden wrench of deceleration jarred through him, putting down his left hand to help brake his momentum. He stopped within a few feet, steadied himself and dropped to one knee. Gabe, anticipating the direction of Sundance's slide and his speed, swung his rifle ahead, squeezing off a shot before he realized the man had stopped.

He swung back towards the pall of dust that half-hid Sundance now, seeing the man taking a bead, and bringing up his own rifle. At the same time that Spooner realized he was exposed from the waist up, Sundance fired two fast shots.

Gabe jarred backwards, one hand clawing at the boulder in an effort to keep from falling. But he was hit too hard. Still he brought his gun over one-handed and fired as Sundance shot again and the lead slammed the ramrod down and out of sight.

Sundance went forward at a steady run, crouched over, rifle across his chest, ready for another shot if necessary.

The girl had ridden back when

she had seen Gabe go down and was kneeling beside the old man whose chest and head were bloody. She glanced up, pale and shaking, as Sundance slowed and saw the blood trickling down Gabe's face. The man's eyes were filled with pain and an abiding hatred. His mouth worked and finally he managed to choke out his last words as Rachel smoothed his forehead with a shaking hand.

"I — shoulda — made a better — job of you — ten years ago . . . " He slumped, coughing, blood spilling from his mouth, and the girl jumped back as some splashed onto her hand.

"Satisfied?" she choked. "You've just killed an old man . . . !"

"The one who murdered my family and left me shot and wounded, then burned my house down around me."

There was no remorse in Sundance, but there was a vast weariness. Then the girl said, "He must've followed me. I saw him with the posse in the pass when I was coming here but I didn't think he'd seen me — and I led him to his death!"

"My God, girl, you're gonna have one helluva life if you insist on taking on guilt this way — you don't make these things happen . . . "

"Will you put him across his horse for me? I — I'll take him back to J-Link-H. It's where he'd want to be buried."

Sundance shook his head wonderingly but did as she asked. She mounted, looked down at him. "I don't suppose killing Gabe will satisfy you . . . ?" His face held the answer to that and she turned her horse's head and touched her spurs to its flanks.

He turned back towards his camp, knowing he would have to get out of here fast now. If she ran into her father and his men, she would lead them back here. She would have to.

★ ★ ★

Morgan Hammer had heard the shooting down in the hidden box canyon but didn't know where it was coming from. But it had had the sounds of a brief and violent gun battle.

Likely it was some of the posse who'd located Sundance. His mouth tightened. He hoped not — he wanted that son of a bitch for himself.

He had been searching for the posse but they must have been deep in the hills or scattered widely. Judging by the sounds of the shooting he'd just heard, it seemed the Reb was hiding in the country on the Cheyenne side of the pass.

He glanced up at the beginning of the pass itself and stiffened when he saw a hunched-over figure up there, clambering over the rocks. Fair hair showed beneath the wide-brimmed hat and . . .

"Man! There *is* a God!" he breathed, hauling rein and sliding his rifle from his scabbard.

That was Sundance up there. What

the hell he was doing there and on foot Morg neither knew nor cared. All he knew was that he had himself a prime target.

He dismounted, rested his arms on the horse, cursing it to a standstill, and drew a careful bead as the figure made his way up into the rocks. Morg's finger caressed the trigger gently and the rifle whiplashed, jarring his shoulder — and he saw the figure up there, balanced on the rim ready to jump into some rocks, suddenly slam forward.

Morg smiled slowly as he levered in a fresh shell and began to hum tunelessly as he mounted and set his dun up the steep, winding trail to the rim. He wanted to yell and dance because he knew he had got his man. *Now* the old man would have to admit he was worth his salt and, with what he knew from reading the journal, Morg would be able to call his own tune from now on. No more being bossed around like a hired hand or being treated like a kid . . .

Then, near the top of the trail he saw the riders just entering the far end of the pass. The posse. Couldn't be better timing. The Colonel was in the lead and . . .

Morg stood in the stirrups and fired his rifle into the air in three evenly spaced shots. He waited a second as the Colonel held up his hand, halting his men, and fired three more times. His father had the direction now and urged the posse on.

Morg reached the top of the trail and dismounted, seeing the head and shoulders of the sprawled figure amongst the rocks. There was blood in the fair hair where the hat lay askew, half covering the face. Then he stiffened as the figure moaned and stirred and turned so that the hat fell off.

"Christ!" Morgan Hammer breathed. It was Kit Dunson!

He went forward. "The name of hell you doin' up here dressed like that! I thought you were Sundance!"

Kit sat up groggily, feeling the bullet crease alongside her head. She stared at him dully, then asked for his neckerchief which she bound around her head. He was still stunned but saw something protruding from her shirt pocket, reached out and snatched it before she could stop him. It was a short length of fuse.

"You bitch! You were gonna blow up the pass! Ah, now I get it, why you're dressed like this and ridin' that chestnut geldin' yonder. You figured if you were seen folk'd think it was Sundance! Like I did."

"What's it to you? You hate his guts."

"Yeah, but I live on the other side of the pass. Hey, you're a mean bitch, ain't you? You sure don't like men runnin' out on you, do you, Kit . . . ?"

"What does that mean?" she asked warily, not liking the smirk on Morg's face.

"I've read pa's journal. I know why you two hate each other now." He

238

waited but Kit stayed silent, tight-lipped. "Seems you and pa had an affair one time when he was on leave. Later, you found out that while you were havin' fun, your husband was dying of his wounds. I guess you never forgave yourself. You sure didn't forgive the Colonel. So you told ma all about it . . . "

"Confessed, rather than told, Morg," Kit said quietly. "I — just had to get it off my chest . . . "

"Well, ma hit the bottle — I can remember some of that, like I remember the blazing arguments when she locked pa outta her bedroom . . . Then, knowin' how much it'd shame him, she ran off with the first Reb drummer to come through after the war. It must've near killed the Colonel."

"Too bad it didn't!" Kit snapped. "I still blame myself for letting it happen but he did all the seducing. After your mother ran off he made it his life's work to destroy me. Fortunately, I'd had enough sense to get Garth Tyson and the other homesteaders to back me up . . . Your father's still trying, Morg, but I don't mean for him to win!"

"You're a pair all right, Kit, you and the Colonel."

They were both startled by the sound of Sundance's voice. He stood beside a tall rock, rifle in hand, sweating from his climb out of the box canyon. He'd heard Morg's gunshots and decided to investigate. Now he said, "You used me all down the line, didn't you, Kit?"

"Well, I did try," she admitted easily. "I'd had hopes of using you to wipe out the Colonel. Or, at least for you to be blamed for it. But Merry and Iliffe put paid to that idea. But now I have another that may work just as well. You were some useful. I did learn how to rig a stick of dynamite by watching you . . . " She smiled crookedly at Morg Hammer, throwing her arms wide. "Let me show you what a good pupil I am, Morg . . . "

Morg frowned but saw Sundance stiffen and swing his rifle slightly in the woman's direction. Morg brought up his own rifle fast and dropped hammer — on an empty chamber. He paled when he swiftly worked the lever and got the same result. He flung the useless weapon at Sundance who was already sliding behind a boulder. Morg palmed up his Peacemaker, threw himself bodily to one side so as to get a better view of Sundance, shooting while still in mid-air. The bullet ripped a line of dust out of the sandstone, the grit stinging Sundance's eyes. He stumbled and Morg fired again. Sundance triggered the rifle blindly, wiping the back of a hand across his eyes.

He jumped off the small ledge to land between two smaller rocks and as he landed, crouching, two of Morg's shots ploughed into the ground in front of him. *Hell, the kid was fast!*

Sundance spread out on his belly, under the overhanging bulge of the boulder. Morg spotted him, fired and ducked as Sundance triggered. Wild with fury now, Morg leapt up with a crazy yell and ran forward, shooting from the hip. With lead whining around him, Sundance worked trigger and lever in three rapid shots, the last fired almost vertically as Morg reached his shelter, leaping onto the rock above. Hammer lifted to his toes, eyes already glazing as he tried one last time to club Sundance with his empty pistol. His legs folded and he sprawled across the rock, his blood staining the sandstone.

Sweating and a mite breathless, Sundance climbed out of the rocks and looked about for Kit. She was nowhere in sight.

Frowning, he went looking for her, gun at the ready, feeling an urgency that twisted up his insides. He hadn't climbed far before he heard her voice, calling from the rim of the pass just beyond a small ridge of broken rock.

"Goodbye, Colonel, you lying son of a bitch! This is the last time anyone gets to use Hellfire Pass!"

"Kit! The other riders!" yelled Sundance as he saw her hunched over a large bundle of dynamite, trying to fire up a match. But the wind was strong up here and blew out the flame. She threw a whitefaced, challenging glance towards Sundance as he started climbing over the broken rock as she fumbled out a fresh vesta.

Sundance stood, pointed to the riders below, the posse, now desperately turning their mounts as they saw what the woman was about. The Colonel had been some yards in the lead and now looked up, groping for his pistol as Kit touched the flaring match to the end of the fuse.

"I might've known you'd be in at the kill, Reb! I never even saw your damn plantation!" His horse turned in an agitated circle and he fought it distractedly. "I just followed orders!"

"You exceeded them, Colonel. And you're yellow — you left it all to your men to do . . . "

In sudden rage, Hammer began firing, lead splintering against rock on the rim, the chips flying. As Kit's arm went back for the throw, she gave a high pitched cry, staggered, and her boot slipped over the broken edge and she tumbled forward, still clutching the explosive. Sundance didn't see her fall, only the thin trailing smoke from the fuse. He twisted and pounded for the rock spine, hurling himself bodily over it as there came a fiery crash of thunder followed by a drum-roll rumbling that set the rock beneath him a'trembling. His ears seemed to implode with the explosion and a fountain of rock and smoke and dirt enveloped him. He felt rather than heard a seemingly endless cannon-fire as thousands of tons of rock crashed and slid down into Hellfire Pass, sealing it forever.

★ ★ ★

After some of the dust settled, he climbed down shakily to where he had left his chestnut, mounted, but kept the animal standing in the shade of the rock walls.

He knew she would be back to investigate the explosion and only minutes later Rachel came riding across the canyon towards him.

She reined down a few yards away, those big, searching eyes drilling into him. *She knows*, he thought. *There isn't anything to say . . .*

But he rode forward and handed her the leather-covered journal. "I have no need of this now, Rachel."

She held it in her small hands and it was a long time before she looked up. Her voice was barely audible and there was contempt mixed with the burning hatred in her eyes. "They're both dead, aren't they?"

"I'm sorry, Rachel."

"No, you're not!" she hissed through her small white teeth. "You've taken your revenge — well, now try to live with it, damn you! I hope you never sleep easy again!"

Her breasts were heaving and tears tracked through the dust on her cheeks. He thought she might faint but the look on her face stopped him from offering assistance. He started to speak, knew it was useless, so bit off the words and lifted the reins, heeling the chestnut forward. "*Adios*, Rachel."

"I'll see you're hounded for murder!" she choked as he touched a hand to his hatbrim. "*For the rest of your life!*"

He put his mount around her and rode slowly across the canyon towards the trail to Cheyenne. The beginning of the long trail that would one day take him all the way back to Texas.

Alone.

THE END

FIGHTING RAMROD
Charles N. Heckelmann

Most men would have cut their losses, but Frazer counted the bullets in his guns and said he'd soak the range in blood before he'd give up another inch of what was his.

LONE GUN
Eric Allen

Smoke Blackbird had been away too long. The Lequires had seized the Blackbird farm, forcing the Indians and settlers off, and no one seemed willing to fight! He had to fight alone.

THE THIRD RIDER
Barry Cord

Mel Rawlins wasn't going to let anything stand in his way. His father was murdered, his two brothers gone. Now Mel rode for vengeance.

ARIZONA DRIFTERS
W. C. Tuttle

When drifting Dutton and Lonnie Steelman decide to become partners they find that they have a common enemy in the formidable Thurston brothers.

TOMBSTONE
Matt Braun

Wells Fargo paid Luke Starbuck to outgun the silver-thieving stagecoach gang at Tombstone. Before long Luke can see the only thing bearing fruit in this eldorado will be the gallows tree.

HIGH BORDER RIDERS
Lee Floren

Buckshot McKee and Tortilla Joe cut the trail of a border tough who was running Mexican beef into Texas. They stopped the smuggler in his tracks.

BRETT RANDALL, GAMBLER
E. B. Mann

Larry Day had the choice of running away from the law or of assuming a dead man's place. No matter what he decided he was bound to end up dead.

THE GUNSHARP
William R. Cox

The Eggerleys weren't very smart. They trained their sights on Will Carney and Arizona's biggest blood bath began.

THE DEPUTY OF SAN RIANO
Lawrence A. Keating and
Al. P. Nelson

When a man fell dead from his horse, Ed Grant was spotted riding away from the scene. The deputy sheriff rode out after him and came up against everything from gunfire to dynamite.